DOOMSDAY MAGIC

LINSEY HALL

For Jon McGough.

1

"Do you really think this will work?" Caro asked as we walked onto the main street in Darklane.

"I hope so." I sidestepped a dodgy-looking character wearing a dark cloak and moved deeper into the black magic neighborhood of Magic's Bend, Oregon.

The sun was beginning to set here, which only served to make the creepy street even creepier. It was creep-squared. The three-story buildings were Victorian in style, but their colorful fronts had been long covered by streaks of dark magic that looked like soot. Even the air smelled dirty here, and the eyes that peered at us from the shadows were not friendly.

Lachlan followed close behind, guarding our backs as we headed toward the Apothecary's Jungle, the shop owned by Aerdeca and Mordaca. We hoped the two Blood Sorceresses would be able to help us.

As we walked, Caro rubbed the tattoo on her palm. I could almost feel her despair radiating toward me. She dropped her hand to her side.

I reached for it and squeezed. "Don't worry, Caro. We'll get that tattoo off of you. The Fates will never make you their slave. We won't let them."

She nodded, her eyes stark. The tattoo had been forcibly applied three days ago, part of an evil plan to control members of the Protectorate. To what end, we had no idea, but it couldn't be good. Over eighty percent of our staff now bore the mark.

It was a huge freaking problem.

Technically, Caro shouldn't have left the security of the Protectorate castle. One step outside of the grounds and the tattoo's spell could ignite, whisking her away to become a slave to the Fates.

Caro dropped my hand. "We have so few of these Seawort protection potions that I feel guilty using one to come see Aerdeca and Mordaca. I hope this works."

"It will."

Caro was our guinea pig. The Protectorate had a few potions that blocked the tattoo's dark magic from stealing her away, and we were banking on the Blood Sorceresses being able to fix Caro. They made house calls, but their magic was strongest here in Darklane. Since we needed some *seriously* strong magic to get out of this bind, we went to them.

The scent of old socks and rotten fruit drifted out of an alley as we passed, and I skirted around to the side, avoiding the noxious smoke that spilled out. Not all dark magic was evil—some of it walked the line—but whatever was going on in there was bad news.

Normally I might peek in to see what was up, but my priority was Caro.

Up ahead, the sign that hung over the Apothecary's Jungle creaked in the wind. Beneath the layer of grime that coated the three-story building, I thought the paint might have once been purple.

"I never thought this part of town suited them," I said.

True, Aerdeca and Mordaca weren't innocent flowers, but they weren't as dark as this place.

"There are parts of them we don't know about, I'm sure," Lachlan said.

I glanced back at him and nodded. "They're enigmas wrapped in riddles wrapped in mysteries and all that."

"Well, thank fates they're here to help, because we're at the end of our line," Caro said.

"It's really weird how we keep thanking the fates while fighting them," I said. "I know it's just a turn of phrase and doesn't mean them specifically, but still, it's weird."

"Totally weird." Caro chuckled and climbed onto the narrow steps that led to their front door.

The air smelled a little bit fresher on their stoop, but that was probably my imagination. I raised my hand and thumped the lion door knocker, then waited.

When the door swung open to reveal Mordaca, I grinned. She was wearing her usual plunging black dress that would put Elvira to shame, and her black bouffant reached at least eight inches toward the ceiling. The black paint that streaked across her eyes looked like a mask, and her lips were red as blood. Her nails were filed to points and painted black.

She played the role of Blood Sorceress perfectly.

Probably because it wasn't a role.

"Good, you're here." She had a pack-a-day smoker's voice and magic that tasted like whisky. "Come in."

We followed her into the small foyer that was tiled in black and white. Cobwebs sat high in the corners, giving the place a real haunted-house feel.

"This way. Aerdeca is waiting." She turned and led us down a short hallway toward their workshop.

Tentatively, I sniffed the air. No black magic smell here,

though there was something slightly off. Magic that walked the borders, probably.

"This place is cool," Caro whispered.

Sorta. Mostly I thought it was a bit creepy, but Aerdeca and Mordaca were our friends, so I wouldn't say it. I didn't have the best manners in the world, but I knew enough to keep my trap shut on that account.

We stepped into a workshop that looked similar to the one Lachlan kept in France. There was a massive wooden table in the middle covered in bowls and knives, along with a few vials of potion. Shelves lined the walls, hundreds of glass bottles glinting in the low light of the fire flickering in the hearth. Herbs hung from the ceiling, delicate plants that waited to be used in their blood magic.

"Good, you're here!" Aerdeca's bird-song voice sounded from behind me, and I turned.

She swept into the room wearing one of her signature white pantsuits, her blonde hair falling like a waterfall over her back. She wore little makeup, and her magic felt like a soft breeze. Like her sister, she wore her nails dagger sharp, but they were painted white.

Both of the sisters were packing a punch today, if I could already feel their magic.

It was tempting to think of Aerdeca as the nice sister—she wore white and sounded so sweet, after all—but that would be a mistake. A *big* mistake.

Neither was sweet.

"Let's see it." Aerdeca walked forward on white stilettos, holding out her hand in an expectant gesture. "I heard you've got a real doozy of a problem."

"That's the truth." Caro stuck out her hand, palm up. Her short platinum hair gleamed in the light of the fire, but her eyes looked tired. Worried.

Aerdeca took her hand and leaned over, her brow creased. Her already pale skin went even whiter. "Yes, this is bad news."

"Let me see." Mordaca budged her sister aside, her long black skirt swishing. She bent low over Caro's hand and squinted, her red lips pursed. Then she looked up at Caro. "Honey, you're in trouble."

"Can you help me?"

"We can try." Mordaca dropped her hand and stepped back. She looked at her sister. "Ready?"

"Let's do this."

They turned and began to pull vials of liquid off the shelves.

Shit.

They didn't even ask about payment. That was *bad* news. The Blood Sorceresses always asked for payment up front. *Always.* I'd heard my friends the FireSouls speak in hushed voices of the times when they didn't mention money.

That's when you knew you had it bad. A problem so big they wanted to solve it without worrying about the green stuff.

Obviously, I didn't mention that to Caro.

Instead, I looked at Lachlan. His dark gaze followed the Blood Sorceresses, concern creasing his brow.

He got it.

For the last three days, he'd done everything he could to figure out what exactly the tattoo did and how to remove it, to no avail. Seers and mages had come to the Protectorate—anyone we'd ever helped—each trying to solve our enormous problem.

No one had had any luck.

Every other Protectorate member was hunting answers, but no one had found any. Yet.

Mordaca turned to us. "Almost ready."

She and her sister each carried a bowl, and their pockets were stuffed full of small vials of potion. They stepped up to the narrow end of the table and pressed their hands to the wood at the corners.

Magic swelled briefly in the air, the taste of whisky and the feel of a breeze. The fire in the hearth flared, and then the table began to move, the massive wooden structure sliding across the floor.

There was nothing unusual underneath it that I could see, but Mordaca and Aerdeca stepped toward the patch of floor that had been revealed by the moving table.

Each sister used one of her dagger-sharp claws to pierce her own finger until blood welled. They held out their hands, letting a tiny droplet fall to the stone floor.

Magic surged again, this time strong enough to blow my hair back and make my throat burn. The stone floor began to shimmer, then it disappeared, revealing a dark staircase that led underground.

"This is why you wanted us to come to Darklane," I said.

Mordaca looked up. "Exactly. Our magic is stronger here because of this. Now, come on."

She and Aerdeca disappeared down the stairs, their heels clicking on the ancient stone.

I followed them, going first and trailing behind Mordaca. The earth smelled damp, and the only light came from a pale green glow up ahead.

It grew brighter as we descended, until finally, I stood on a little platform, facing a wall of glowing green vines. They blocked our path, moving like snakes, shifting and slithering over each other.

I shivered. "Wait, *are* those? Snakes?"

"They're called ærlig vines," Mordaca said. "They make sure that no one breaks in."

A vine reached out and slapped against me, hard enough to sting. Another reached for my wrist and tightened around me.

"Hey!" I tried to pull back, but it only tightened further.

"Calm down," Mordaca said. "It just wants a drop of your blood."

"Oh, that's all." I scowled at her, then called a dagger from the ether.

It appeared in my free hand, and I gripped the hilt, turning the blade so I could prick the finger of my bound hand. Pain pinched briefly, then the blood welled. Next to me, Lachlan and Caro did the same, each drawing a tiny drop of blood.

"Do exactly as we do." Aerdeca pressed her still-bleeding finger onto a particularly fat vine.

The bright green plant slithered back, and its fellows followed, creating a gap in the vines. Aerdeca stepped through, disappearing into the morass. It closed behind her immediately, opening again when Mordaca did the same.

The vine that wrapped around my wrist was squeezing tighter, and my fingertips were starting to tingle. "You guys mind if I go next? I want this thing to let me go."

"I sure as heck don't want to go first," Caro said.

Lachlan nodded.

I turned my bleeding finger toward the vine and pressed it to the slick surface. Immediately, the pressure on my wrist loosened, and the vines slipped away from the space in front of me, slithering back to reveal a narrow passage.

I sucked in a breath and stepped into the darkness. The vines reached out to slap at me as I passed through, one landing right on my butt.

"Hey! Quit being handsy, vine."

The vine slithered back, as if it understood me.

Okay, that was actually even creepier.

A moment later, I stepped out into the stairwell, which continued downward. Aerdeca and Mordaca waited for us, and once Lachlan and Caro had made it through, we continued down.

The path ahead continued to glow, this time with a faint yellow light. We followed the spiral deeper, and by the time we reached it, the glow was so bright that I had to squint.

"Are they fairy lights?" Caro asked.

I squinted at them. She had a point. They looked a lot like the fairy lights that glittered in the Enchanted Forest back at the Protectorate castle.

"Lights of Truth," Mordaca said. "Answer their question and they'll let you through."

Aerdeca stepped into the little lights, which zipped around her head, flying through the air like fairy lights on speed. Voices began to murmur through the stairs, a language I didn't recognize.

How the heck was I supposed to answer questions in a language I didn't speak? I'd opened my mouth to ask when Aerdeca disappeared, absorbed by the lights. Mordaca followed, vanishing so quickly that she was gone in the space of a few heartbeats.

"Well, crap," Caro said. "I don't speak *light*."

"Aye, not fluent myself," Lachlan said.

"Me neither." I frowned, then stepped forward, hoping for the best.

Immediately, warmth surrounded me. The lights flitted closer, brushing my skin and leaving behind a trail of heat. The voices began to murmur in my ears, unrecognizable at first.

Then something in them coalesced. A common thread of sound that began to form words.

Do you have the permission of Aerdeca and Mordaca to enter their sacred space?

"Um, yes?" I said. "They led us here, so I figure that counts."

Do you mean harm?

I thought about it. "To some, yes." I'd kill the Fates without hesitation. Tear their heads right off. "But not to Mordaca and Aerdeca."

The lights seemed to like that answer, because they buzzed excitedly then pushed me through. Heat flared against my back wherever they touched me, and soon, I was in the spiral stairwell with Aerdeca and Mordaca.

Aerdeca looked at Mordaca. "See, I knew she was legit."

"Totally not an asshat."

A laugh almost burst out of me at the sound of the ever-so-elegant Aerdeca using the word *asshat.* "I have my moments."

Caro appeared behind me, the lights ejecting her from their domain. She grinned. "Cool security system."

Lachlan followed a moment later.

"Three out of three ain't bad," Mordaca said.

"I should hope they'd all make it through," Aerdeca said. "Else we'd have made a serious error in judgement."

"We would *never.*" Mordaca sounded aghast.

I chuckled.

They led us down the spiral staircase, moving quickly in the dim light.

"We're nearly there," Aerdeca said. "No more security."

When we reached an underground chamber at the base of the stairs, the scent of water was even stronger. I exited the stairwell and spotted a pool of pale blue water in the middle of the dark space. It was about twenty feet across and looked like it'd been carved from the dirt thousands of years ago. The glow from the water lit up the space as it glittered invitingly, and a wave of magic rolled off of it.

I gasped at the feeling it emitted. "That's strong magic. No wonder you choose to live in Darklane."

"Well, we also like the culture." Mordaca's expression was

deadpan. "But it took us ages to find this well of power. They're very rare. This is the only one in Oregon."

"And conveniently, it's located right in Magic's Bend," Aerdeca said.

"It may be one of the reasons Magic's Bend was founded here, actually," Mordaca said. "We bought the place from an old witch who wanted to retire to Florida and play canasta."

"Canasta?" I asked.

"I don't know." Aerdeca shrugged elegantly. "Some kind of game. Old witches love it. Anyhow, we signed a document promising we'd reveal its existence only when necessary, and only to those we trust. You passed the test, so evidently, we were right to trust you."

"We conduct our most difficult magic down here." Mordaca nodded toward Caro's hand. "And *that* is some difficult magic."

Caro raised her hand and glared at it. "I just want it off me."

"I can't say that I blame you." Aerdeca gestured us forward. "Come, step into the water."

Caro obeyed, and I followed, wanting a better look.

Aerdeca held up her hand. "Only Caro. It's too dangerous for you to touch the water while we conduct our spell. Only those who *must* stand within it should do so."

I stopped in my tracks, a few feet from the edge of the glittering pond. This close, the magic was even stronger, a powerful signature that felt like waves crashing over me. It reminded me of Arach, the dragon spirit who lived at the Protectorate castle.

Lachlan came to stand next to me as Caro stepped into the water, joining Aerdeca and Mordaca, who stood submerged up to their knees. Mordaca's black dress floated around her, rippling gently.

I tried not to make a peep as the Blood Sorceresses began to work. They stood in front of Caro, who watched with wide eyes as they pulled vials from their pockets and poured them into a little bowl that they'd brought. Aerdeca bent to scoop some water into the bowl, and whatever was within it began to smoke profusely. The little plumes that wafted off the surface were the deep red of blood.

As the final touch, each sorceress poked her finger with a fingernail and added a single drop of real blood to the mix. The smoke turned orange, then ceased completely.

"This might sting a bit," Aerdeca said.

"Don't listen to her. She's a wimp." Mordaca grinned.

Aerdeca's elbow twitched, and she clearly wanted to jab it into her sister's side, but she held the bowl of potion. She glanced at it, then resisted the urge. "You're lucky I don't want to spill." Her gaze met Caro's. "We're going to paint runes on your skin with this. If it works as planned, it will reveal who created the spell that is imbued in that tattoo. With any luck, we'll be able to remove it."

Caro nodded, seeming both stalwart and anxious, which was a difficult combo to pull off.

Aerdeca's gaze became serious. "Whatever happens, do not go any deeper into the water."

She didn't elaborate, but she didn't need to. Her tone made it obvious something would happen.

Something awful.

Death.

Mordaca dug a slender paintbrush out of her pocket. How she managed to fit so many pockets in such a sleek dress, I had no idea. Magic swelled on the air as she dipped the brush into the potion and began to paint it onto Caro's outstretched arms. It tasted like Mordaca's whiskey signature and felt like the cool breeze of Aerdeca's, but with something else layered over the top. Something slightly dark from the way it prickled across my skin.

The blue pond glittered more fiercely as the paint was applied, magic making the surface ripple.

Caro grimaced, then stiffened her spine.

Moments passed, and the magic in the air began to strengthen. Blue steam rose off the surface of the water, then began to swirl around the three women. It seeped into my lungs, burning slightly.

I blinked, my vision going hazy through the smoke as my lungs continued to ache.

Caro cried out, sharp and intense.

Then she fell, dropping backward.

Aerdeca shouted, panic in her voice.

Don't go any deeper into the water. Their warning flashed in my mind, along with the deadly consequences.

I lunged forward, reaching for Caro, hoping to catch her. As soon as my foot splashed into the water, magic exploded outward. The explosive force came directly from Caro, slamming into me and making my hand burn like crazy.

"No!" Mordaca screamed.

My heart thudded. She'd never sounded so frightened.

It was the last thing I heard before a massive force tugged at my ankles, pulling me into the water. It closed around my head, stinging fiercely against my skin. Panic closed my throat as I scrabbled for the surface, trying to claw my way upward. But it was no good. I kept going deeper.

2

The water pulled at me, dragging me deeper. Something *else* pulled at me, something that came from far away. It tore at my muscles, tugging and yanking. My muscles felt like they would tear away from my bones, and agony streaked through me.

Bubbles whirled as I tried to fight my way to the surface, but I was too weak. Too broken. All of my flailing did no good.

Through bleary vision, I thought I saw shapes above the water. Someone dragging Caro back—I could identify her silvery, platinum hair—then another, diving for me.

It was the last thing I saw as the agony made my vision go black. The force tried to tear me away, like the ether when it sucked me into a portal. I fought it, instinct compelling me to resist with every fiber of my being.

I didn't want to go wherever this force was trying to take me.

Strong hands gripped my arms, yanking me through the water. The pain flared brighter.

"No!" I tried to scream, but only bubbles escaped my mouth.

I didn't want to be dragged away, but being saved made the pain worse. Whoever was trying to rescue me was fighting the force that tried to pull me away, and it tore at my muscles and bones all the fiercer.

They didn't stop, though, pulling and yanking me through the water until my head burst through the surface. I sucked air into my lungs, gasping raggedly.

The pain.

Out of the water, I could feel the hot tears rolling down my face. But I could barely see. What was wrong with my vision?

"I've got you." Lachlan's rough voice broke through the haze.

I tried to talk but could only croak. No real words escaped my mouth.

"Get her upstairs!" Aerdeca's voice sounded. "Now!"

I was moving then, jostling in Lachlan's arms as he raced up the stairs.

"Hurry!" Mordaca shouted. "She's not protected! The spell is still trying to drag her away!"

Panic flared. My heart thundered so hard it felt like it was beating against my aching muscles. Fear like I'd never known filled me, an icy chill that did nothing to numb the pain.

"Put her on the table!"

Who was speaking? I could no longer see. I think I tried to writhe in pain, but I couldn't control my body anymore.

"Hold on to her!" someone screamed. "Don't let go or they'll get her."

They?

Who?

The Fates.

It was the only rational thought in my head, and I knew it was driven by fear.

It hurt so bad I wanted to tell Lachlan to let me go. If he did, maybe the pain would stop. I tried to speak, but no words came.

Something flashed in my mind, dark and quick.

I latched onto it. Any distraction from this pain was welcome.

A crow.

It was a massive crow, flying through my mind. The wings were a bright, shiny black as the bird soared.

A sense of control flowed through me. The pain was still there. The panic, too.

But somehow, I could get control of it.

I clung to the sensation, keeping my eye on the crow as it swept in front of my eyes. It was my lifeline, and I clung to it.

Slowly, part of my brain returned to the present. It was just a sliver, and I still couldn't see, but I could make out movement around me. Frantic bustling from the people surrounding me.

Then pain, flaring sharp at my palm. A cut?

It burned, just briefly.

Then sweet relief began to flow. The absence of pain. Better than any kind of pleasure, when it just stopped *hurting.*

The painless bliss streamed up my arm to my chest, then down my other limbs and through my head, bringing with it a sense of calm.

Finally, the pain was all gone.

I blinked, my vision slowly clearing.

Lachlan, Caro, Aerdeca, and Mordaca all stood over me, staring down. Their faces were all whiter than snow, their eyes stark.

"Are you all right?" Lachlan's voice was rough.

"Do you still feel the pulling sensation?" Mordaca demanded. Her eyes raced over me, her lips tight.

"No," I croaked. "I don't feel it." Aching, I tried to sit. Was I on the big table in their workshop?

Yes. I gripped the sides.

"Let me help you." Lachlan reached behind my back and

helped me sit, his strong arms giving my weak muscles the strength they needed to move.

"What happened?" My voice was almost a whisper, and I felt like I could use a nap for a century. "Are you all okay?"

"You saved Caro," Mordaca said. "But you screwed yourself."

Relief flashed through me, followed by dread. "What do you mean?"

"She was about to fall into the water, and you caught her," Aerdeca said. "The spell that we'd placed on her to learn the origin of the tattoo weakened her system enough that she wouldn't have survived a dip in the pool. But when you stepped into the water, the magic that imbued her tattoo transferred to you, too."

"Like a virus." Mordaca's eyes were grim.

"What?" It was exhausting agony to speak the words, and only Lachlan's arms were keeping me upright.

"The water is a conduit for our magic, making it flow stronger and fiercer," Mordaca said. "It was also a conduit for the spell."

Aerdeca lifted my hand, the one that had so recently been burning. She turned it so I could see the palm.

The tattoo stared back at me. A cross with a circle around it.

Just like the one Caro wore.

"Holy fates." Horror streaked through me.

"As soon as you received the tattoo, it started to drag you away from here. You aren't wearing the same protective amulet that Caro is wearing."

"That's what the tearing sensation was."

"Exactly." Aerdeca nodded. "The spell ages over time. It was given to Caro several days ago, so it's had that amount of time to grow. It wasn't that strong when she first received it."

"But why did the spell act so strongly on Ana if she just received it?" Lachlan asked.

"It wasn't really a fresh tattoo, though it seems like it is," Mordaca said. "It's part of Caro's tattoo, magically transferred. So it began to drag her away immediately. Given time, it will only become stronger. It will tear you away so fast you won't realize that it's happened until you're a captive of the Fates."

"But I'm protected now?" I peered at my palm, my stomach turning.

"For about a week, yes," Aerdeca said. "We made you a quick binding charm. It won't last forever, though."

"And it used up our supply of Mugwort." Mordaca frowned, then seemed to catch herself and winked at me. "Worth it for you, though."

"So you can't make another, is what you mean," Lachlan said. "Ana has a week, then she'll become a captive of the Fates."

"Precisely," Mordaca said.

"Unless she hides out at the Protectorate castle, like the rest of us," Caro said.

The two Blood Sorceresses nodded.

I swallowed hard. It was no way to live, hiding out at the castle. Worse, one day the Fates might attack. If they succeeded, we'd lose our protection and become their slaves anyway.

Shit, this was bad news.

"But you are lucky," Aerdeca said. "The Mugwort potion will allow you to use your magic. It's stronger than Seawort, the potion that is protecting Caro and some of the other Protectorate members."

That was lucky, at least. Seawort protected Caro and the others from being dragged away by the spell, but their magic was still dampened. Part of the tattoo's curse suppressed their magic. They could only use it if the Fates allowed it, and of course they didn't. I was grateful to have mine, though. Exhaustion dragged at my eyes as I tried to keep them open. It was the kind of tired that physically hurt.

I forced myself to speak. "Did you figure out anything about the tattoo?"

Please say yes. Considering how wrong this had gone, I prayed we had at least a few answers.

"Yes," Aerdeca said. "Just before you were taken, we learned who made the spell that imbues it."

"Not the Fates?" Caro asked.

I was glad she knew the right questions to ask, because speaking had nearly become too much for me.

"Not them. It's too advanced," Aerdeca said. "It was made by a cult of people who live far to the north. The Indomidae. You can access them through the Corryvreckan whirlpool."

Lachlan frowned. "A whirlpool?"

"One of the few that exists naturally," Mordaca said. "It is now a portal. If you can reach it, you will find the Indomidae. They can tell you how to remove the tattoos."

"Which means you can't tell us." Dejection sounded in Caro's voice.

Mordaca shook her head. "Unfortunately, no. Their magic is closely guarded, but it carries a distinct signature."

"The scent of salt air and the feel of a seal's sleek pelt across your palm," Aerdeca said. "Impossible to mistake. But if you find them, and somehow manage to get the information, you might be able to remove those tattoos."

Might.

That was a terrible word.

It was the last thought I had before exhaustion made me slump on the table.

THE DREAM *FELT* LIKE A DREAM. That kind of hazy reality that was almost the truth, but you knew it wasn't.

I walked over the rock-strewn hillside, the wind tearing at my hair. Heavy black clouds roiled on the horizon, blocking out the sun and sending the day into an early dusk. The air was chill, tugging at my skirts.

Skirts?

I looked down, catching sight of the heavy green wool that flapped around my legs. Golden embroidery covered the bottom, beautiful in its ornate delicacy. Old-fashioned-looking leather boots peeped out from beneath the hem of the skirt with every step I took, the toes pointed.

"What the heck am I wearing?" I muttered, holding out my arms to stare at the long, tight sleeves of the dress. The same emerald green, accented with golden thread.

Something was slung across my back, and I reached to grab it and pull it around to the front.

A bow, beautifully carved of golden wood, with Celtic knots inscribed in the gleaming surface. More exploration revealed a quiver of arrows.

I'd never favored the bow and arrow. If anyone did, it was Rowan, but even she didn't use it exclusively. The heavy golden belt at my waist was fitted with a dagger, long and sharp. But somehow, I knew I used the bow more often.

I kept walking, wondering where I was going while simultaneously feeling like I had an important destination in mind.

But I was all the way out in the middle of nowhere. Just rolling hills and rocks. Every now and again, a barren oak tree reached for the thundering sky, skinny branches quivering in the breeze.

Overhead, crows circled, shiny black birds that weaved through the clouds.

I felt a kinship with them, almost like they were family.

Almost like *I* was a crow.

Um, nah.

That was nuts. I wasn't a shifter. And would I really choose a *crow*?

From high overhead, the birds cawed, as if they were offended. Smart bastards.

I reached the top of the hill and hung my bow over a branch of the barren oak tree that held a lonely vigil. It was odd to observe my motions, almost as if I weren't part of them. I was doing them, but *not*.

I removed the quiver next, then my belt and dagger. A half second later, magic surged through me, bright and fierce. It felt like nothing familiar. Not like my magic, at least.

Every nerve ending buzzed, as if champagne were flowing through my veins.

Then I leapt from the ground, flying high into the air.

Flying?

But I was. The earth fell away below me, the tree growing smaller with every flap of my wings.

Holy fates, I had wings.

I looked left and right, catching sight of the bright black wings that carried me through the air. The crows began to circle around me, tiny in comparison to my bulk.

I was big!

And I was a *crow*.

Strangely, the greatest sense of power flowed through me. Battle cries sounded in the distance, the clash of steel. It was my domain. I could feel it.

I could fly to the battle and smite one side, forcing them to lose.

It was all up to me, if I wanted it to be.

Instead, I swooped through the sky, joy alighting in my chest at the feel of the wind in my feathers. The clouds were no longer threatening. They were my playground.

What the hell was I?

An answer echoed in my mind, though I had no idea where it came from.

Warrior goddess. Battle Crow.

I woke in my bed, my mouth tasting like old fish and death. I couldn't breathe. A horrible weight crushed my chest. My lungs didn't work.

Gasping in a ragged breath, I opened my eyes.

Muffin stared down at me, his ugly wrinkled face only a few inches from mine. Concern flashed in his green eyes, and he breathed gently on me, whiskers quivering.

I gagged. "You have tuna breath."

I found a can, but there's none left for you. Are you all right?

"How'd you open it?" I croaked.

He held up one paw and extended a single gleaming claw. *I have my ways.*

"Remind me not to get on your bad side." Hardly able to breathe because his big butt was pinning me to the bed, I nudged him off of me.

He ambled onto the bed, wobbling a bit on the fluffy covers, then turned back to me. *Are you all right? You look pale. Smell weird, too.*

"I wouldn't be accusing people of smelling weird, Tuna Breath."

One man's trash is another cat's tuna. He butted me with his head, being strangely affectionate.

"Jeez, I must really be in bad shape if you're being so nice."

You look bad.

Memories crashed into me. The visit to Darklane, the pool beneath the earth, Caro's tattoo. *My* tattoo.

I raised my hand and looked at it, dread coursing through me.

The dark symbol marred my hand, and I swallowed hard. "I was hoping it'd been a bad dream."

I'd barely been conscious through most of it. Turns out, that didn't matter.

Muffin hissed at the tattoo. *Bad news.*

"No kidding." I scrambled up and raced toward the bathroom, not sure if I were going to hurl or throw myself into the shower.

I chose the shower, cranking up the water to high heat. My skin itched all over, probably from my dip in that horrible pool. Within seconds, I'd torn off my clothes and jumped in the water. I scrubbed ferociously at my hand, to no avail.

You could cut it off.

I looked up at the sound of Muffin's voice. He sat on the bar that held the shower curtain, wobbling slightly to keep his balance. His little wings fluttered, giving him some extra staying power.

"Hedy isn't sure that will work." We'd already explored that avenue. No one wanted to chop their hand off, of course, but if it kept them from becoming slaves to the Fates, they were willing to try. "She said that there's a chance the spell is already part of us. The tattoo is the base and helped it get into us, but the spell was probably placed on our whole bodies. So we could chop our hands off and still be screwed."

Muffin scrunched up his face. *Not good. How will you open tuna?*

"No kidding." I made quick work of scrubbing the rest of myself clean, then I hopped out and tugged on clothes. A quick glance in the mirror showed that Muffin was right.

I looked bad.

So pale that the golden torc tattoo stood out starkly on my

collarbones, and my eyes were dark. Nearly black, which was weird.

Black as a crow's feathers.

I staggered, bracing myself against the bathroom sink.

Holy fates, *the dream.*

I hadn't remembered it at first, not with the stress of discovering the tattoo. But now I did.

What did it mean?

Just the idea of trying to unpack all the symbolism in the dream made me tired. I didn't have time for it. Not now. Not when we maybe had a clue about the tattoos.

I needed to find the others.

I rushed out of the apartment, passing a conked-out Bojangles and Princess Snowflake III. Three open tuna cans sat on my counter, so they were clearly in a food coma.

I found everyone in the round room, as I'd expected. It was packed with people, most of them standing against the walls. Nearly everyone had a tattoo—over eighty percent of the staff had been abducted last week and given the terrible, cursed artwork. They couldn't leave the castle, and while they did what they could in the library and armory to stay useful, there was still a sense of frustration that filled the air.

Even Arach was there, the ghostly dragon spirit presiding over the meeting in her near-human form. Her gaze was solemn as she watched the proceedings.

If Arach was at a meeting, you knew it was a big deal.

There were only about a dozen of us who could leave the castle grounds, plus the FireSouls, who'd agreed to help us look for a cure. Everyone who could leave the castle had set off, searching for other clues, trying to find the answer to the riddle of the terrible tattoo.

Jude stopped talking and looked up at me, her eyes brightening. "Ana! Are you okay?"

"Fine."

Lachlan's eyes searched me, concern glinting in their depths. He rose, and I nodded at him.

"I'm fine." I took the only seat left at the table, next to Lachlan and my sisters. "Where are we?"

"Everyone else is off hunting their own leads," Jude said. "But it sounds like you, Lachlan, and Caro discovered something. You're going to go find the Indomidae and see what they know. You can leave whenever you're ready. I've given Lachlan instructions."

"I can leave the castle grounds?" I asked, raising my hand to show the tattoo.

"Mordaca and Aerdeca assured us that the Mugwort potion they gave you would protect you for up to a week," Lachlan said. "But if you prefer not—"

"No, no, I want to go. I just forgot." I rubbed my head, trying to bring back other memories. It was all hazy, cloaked in memories of pain and fear. "Let's go. I want to figure this the hell out."

Lachlan squeezed my arm. "I thought you'd say that."

The meeting ended a moment later. I stood, along with Lachlan and my sisters, and looked at them. "Looks like I missed all the boring bits."

Rowan laughed, her dark hair gleaming. "Hardly."

"Good work with Aerdeca and Mordaca," Bree said. "That's our first solid clue in days. The FireSouls almost found something yesterday, but no go. The clue was a dead end."

"Damn." I really hoped this panned out for us, then. "Where are you guys off to?"

"Jude found a contact in Darklane who has more Seawort," Bree said.

"Really? That's great." Seawort was the primary ingredient in the potion that allowed people with the tattoo to leave the castle grounds. It couldn't give them their magic back like the super rare Mugwort potion could, but it was valuable all the same.

"We're off to get some," Rowan said. "We need to increase the number of people who can leave. Not just to find the cure for this tattoo curse, but to defend the castle if the Fates ever find us and decide to attack."

It was our greatest fear. If the castle walls fell, anyone with the tattoo would immediately become their slave. We needed that potion to protect them if that happened. Only then would we have the numbers we needed to fight back. The Seawort potion only lasted about a week, but that was long enough to fight off the Fates if they attacked the castle. Or die trying.

"Good luck finding enough Seawort for everyone." I hugged them both. "Be careful."

"You too." Bree looked at Lachlan. "Watch out for our girl, all right?"

"I'm pretty sure she'll watch out for me."

I grinned, then waved goodbye to my sisters, who hurried off down the hall. I turned to Lachlan. "I want to go see the Indomidae alone. It's too dangerous—you could end up with a cursed tattoo of your own."

His gaze turned serious. "I'm coming, Ana."

"I really don't think you should."

"You're worth the risk."

Warmth spread from my heart to my cheeks.

He squeezed my hand. "I mean it, Ana."

I nodded. "All right, then. What exactly is on our agenda?"

"We're headed to a town in the far northwest of Scotland where we can catch a boat that will take us to the whirlpool portal."

I led the way out of the room, turning to look at him as we walked down the hall. "Why don't you sound excited about that?"

"It's an all-demon city."

"Demonville?" I'd only ever heard of it, but the stories weren't good.

"Aye. Jude assures me that the demons won't attack us outright. She said that there's a person there called the Seamstress who will help us. Jude said she's a good one to visit—that she often gives a great deal of help."

The Seamstress was a weird name, but I tabled that for a more pressing matter. "Why can't we just get a boat from here? We're on the far north coast."

"We need a guide. And the North Sea is incredibly dangerous. It's safer if we depart from Demonville. It's closer to the whirlpool."

"Fair enough." We stepped into the entry hall, and my stomach grumbled. "Let's swing by the kitchen and grab something to go. I'm famished."

As if he'd read my mind, Hans stepped out of the door that led to the kitchen stairs, two paper sacks in his hands. His eyes brightened at the sight of us, and his mustache quivered. "Just the people I was looking for!"

I grinned. "I could say the same about you."

He thrust out two bags. "Sandwiches and juice boxes for the road."

I took them. "Thanks, Hans."

"Good luck out there." His normally jovial expression was serious, his face grim. Even Boris, who I now spotted sitting on top of his chef's hat, had a downturn to his whiskers.

"We'll figure this out," I said. "Promise."

Under any circumstances, I'd give it my all. But now? Even *I* had the tattoo. This fight had already been personal, but they'd taken it up a notch.

We said goodbye to Hans and departed, eating our sandwiches as we walked to the edge of the castle courtyard, where Lachlan normally created his portals.

Lachlan stopped and turned to me. "Ready?"

"As I'll ever be."

"Good, because this is going to be dangerous."

I had a feeling that was the understatement of the century.

3

Lachlan's portal spit us out at the edge of a town. I blinked. It was one of the creepiest places I'd ever been. A dark cloud seemed to hover around it, and the sun was so deep in the clouds that the day looked like dusk.

I glanced at Lachlan. "This place scares the sun itself."

"Aye, it's not for the fainthearted."

A sea breeze blew salty air, bringing with it the scent of weeds and dead fish. In the distance, the sound of waves crashed, but we were situated behind a slight hill, so I couldn't see the ocean. The town was pressed right against it, however, so far at the edge of the world that it felt like the only town on the planet.

"We sure know how to pick them," Lachlan said.

"Between this and the fairy tale village, we've been doing an extensive tour of creepy places." I searched the backs of the houses that sat on the outskirts of town, looking for movement. I saw none. "Let's go check it out."

"Aye."

We approached the town. As we passed the row of outermost houses, a prickle of dark magic fizzed across my skin. I shivered.

"Yep, definitely a demon city," I muttered.

"I'm surprised there are no guards," Lachlan said.

"Who would want to come here?"

"Fair point. It's miserable as hell and at the end of the world."

I studied the buildings as we passed them. Most looked like really old cottages. The building styles were a collection of different periods, from medieval—which I recognized because it really did look like it was from a fairy tale—to the simpler, more modern nineteenth-century cottages. A few even had flowers growing outside, though they were all in shades of black or gray. Even the roses and daisies were colorless.

After a couple rows of houses, we entered the main town. The buildings pressed up against each other, rising two and three stories tall. The street was cobbled and narrow, winding between the buildings.

Rats scurried underfoot, more than I'd ever seen out in the open before. One of them turned to me and hissed, its yellow teeth glinting under the light of an oil street lamp.

"Good day to you, too," I said.

The rat hissed again and scurried away, its little tail bobbing as he raced up a darkened alleyway.

"I bet he's the friendliest figure we meet all day," I said.

"Given a place like this, aye."

"That hiss was almost a greeting."

"A how-do-you-do."

I grinned at him, delighted despite our dark surroundings. I liked that he could joke about a rat with me. It was ridiculous and wonderful.

We passed a pub next, and the joking faded. It was heaving with patrons from the sound of it, and I squinted through the window. The room within was filled with golden light, and it should have been a homey sight. It was, for the millisecond before I noticed all the horns and fangs.

Everyone in the building was a demon.

I shivered.

"Never been so close to so many demons without intending to start a fight," I said.

"More like finish a fight, since they're the ones who usually start them."

"Good point. Let's move on." So far, the streets had been delightfully empty. "I'd rather find the Seamstress on our own, or at least ask a solo demon for directions. I'm not keen on hanging out with dozens of them."

"Agreed," Lachlan said.

Jude had said they wouldn't kill us outright, but I had a smart mouth. I couldn't guarantee that *something* wouldn't get started. And with that many demons, our victory wasn't certain.

We hurried on, canvassing the streets for the Seamstress's shop. We passed a few demons, but each crossed the street to avoid us. Even they weren't really comfortable here.

Finally, we ran into a demon who didn't cross the street. He leaned against a shop building, smoking a cigarette that smelled like old weeds.

He was big and burly, about Lachlan's size, but broader. Which was saying something, since Lachlan wasn't a skinny guy. The demon's horns were about a foot long and decorated with silver wire. His burnished red skin was complemented by jet-black eyes, and he looked like a perfect version of the devil. I wanted to ask if he had a forked tail, but kept my mouth shut. That would be a *bad* idea.

His black gaze traveled up and down our forms. "Not from around here."

I turned to him. "Nope. Got any idea where the Seamstress is?"

"Why would you want to see her?"

"Got my reasons. Do you know?"

"I might know." His eyes flicked down toward our pockets.

Lachlan got the hint before I did and reached into his pocket to tug out some money.

Ah, right. Bribery.

I grinned at the demon. "So you do know where she is."

He held out his hand. Lachlan put a fifty-pound note in it.

"I know now," the demon said. "Head up the street to Warlock Road and take a right. She's the fourth building down on the right. You won't miss it."

"Thanks." I nodded.

"But cross the street here. You don't want to walk in front of the Necro's door." He pointed up the street.

"What's the Necro?" Lachlan asked.

He grinned a fangy smile, then stubbed out his cigarette on the stone wall behind him. "You'll figure it out."

With that, he pushed off the wall and went back into the building.

I looked at Lachlan. "I don't think we want to figure it out."

"Aye. Let's cross the street."

We did as the demon advised, but I kept my eyes glued to the side of the road where the Necro was located.

The stink in the air grew stronger as we approached, taking on the unmistakable odor of death.

Understanding dawned. "Ah crap. The Necro is a necromancer."

"Aye, that makes sense."

The windows were full of body parts. *Actual flipping body parts.*

I shuddered. "Looks like a horror movie."

Lachlan grabbed my hand and tugged me along. "Don't look."

I dragged my gaze away from the display window and trudged up the street, going as fast as I could without breaking into a run. Something told me that if you started running in this town, the locals would get *real* interested. Like the way a dog started chasing a cat if it began to run.

I was not going to be the cat. Especially not if the necromancer was chasing me.

We came to Warlock Road and turned right, striding down the narrow lane. The second house that we passed was built entirely of bone.

I stopped dead, staring at it. There were thousands of bones, maybe millions, all pressed tightly together and held in place by mortar.

"Holy fates," I muttered. "Look at that."

"Aye, hard to miss it."

A voice whispered out from the house, creaky and light. "They're all ethically sourced."

I stifled a laugh. "Like from a murderous farmers' market?"

The voice didn't answer, and we'd lingered long enough. I started onward again. We should be nearly there.

As the smoking demon had said, the building was the fourth on the right. Two stories and built of a rustic dark wood, it didn't look particularly creepy. The sign above the door said The Seamstress, and it was decorated with swirling thread that twisted around it.

"Well, it's obvious at least." I rapped on the door, hoping she was home.

A few moments later, it creaked open, revealing a tiny woman with grayish skin. Her dark hair was shiny and bright, her eyes a brilliant green. Tiny horns popped out of her hair, and each was inset with an emerald that matched her eyes. Her long green dress looked impeccably made, even to me, who knew nothing about clothes. A few pieces of spare cloth hung over her shoulder, like she'd been in the middle of working.

"Yes?" Her voice was light and curious, her eyes sharp.

"We need help."

She held up a hand. "Say no more. Come in."

Okay, that was easy. I glanced at Lachlan. He shrugged and nodded.

Warily, I stepped inside. Normally it *wasn't* this easy. I didn't trust it. But I also didn't have any other options. The tattoo on my hand burned, reminding me that I didn't have a lot of time.

The front entry to the building was cramped and small, but the room behind was a heck of a lot larger than I'd expected. It was dimly lit, but every inch was covered in fabric, and mannequins stood like sentries, each wearing a different outfit. They were all intricate works of art that had to take weeks to make.

Movement rustled through the space, fabric shifting and spools of thread floating through the air. I squinted, finally realizing that it was caused by rats and birds, each moving amongst the material, thread and scissors gripped in their jaws and claws.

"They're my helpers," the Seamstress said.

"Like Cinderella."

She laughed. "She's a goody-two-shoes copycat, and she knows it."

I turned to her, a slightly weirded-out smile on my face. I liked this place. "Can you help us—"

She held up a hand again, cutting me off. "No, no. We do it my way."

"Okay?"

She bustled up to me, three rats following in her wake. One carried a measuring tape, the loose end trailing behind it. Another carried a pair of scissors. The final carried a little leather folder.

"Up there." The Seamstress pointed to a footstool.

I climbed onto it, my gaze never leaving the Seamstress.

She walked around me, tapping her lip with her fingertip and humming to herself. "Let's see, let's see. What do you need?"

The rats squeaked and the birds chirped.

"Ah, yes." The Seamstress nodded. "You need a jacket."

I looked down at the leather jacket I wore. I quite liked it. "Really?"

"Really. You live a dangerous life. I can see that. Therefore, you need a better jacket."

I didn't see how a jacket would help me with my dangerous life. Nor did I see how this was getting us any closer to the whirlpool that would take us to the Indomidae. "Um, but what about—"

She held up her hand again, and I shut my mouth, only belatedly realizing that I hadn't *chosen* to shut my mouth. I hadn't noticed last time, but this time, I definitely freaking noticed. It was damned frustrating.

"You'll see in time," she said. "But I can only help you if we do it my way."

I nodded, reluctantly satisfied. Bemused, I watched her get to work. She measured me first, her motions so quick that the measuring tape almost flew through the air, whipping around me.

All the while, she muttered to herself. Then she cut the fabric, the whole process taking less than a minute. I'd never seen anyone move quite so fast. The whole time, the rats and birds helped her.

The last step was to sew the jacket, which she did, her hands flying so quickly I could hardly see them. There were a few parts still held together with pins when she turned, grinning, and held it out. "Try it on."

I shrugged out of my old jacket and tossed it to Lachlan, then took the new one and put it on. Immediately, I felt stronger. Braver, too. I could go shut down that necromancer right now.

I shook myself, blinking. "Whoa."

"It just needs a few little nips and tucks." She bustled around me, pins stuck in her mouth, adjusting and changing. Then she began to sew. She'd made a few stitches when the needle leapt from her hand and flew into the air, hovering right in front of my face.

I squeezed my eyes shut, raising my hands to protect them.

She laughed. "It's not a threat. We're really getting down to business, now."

Wary, I split my fingers apart and peeked through the gap.

The needle had begun to dance in the air, the thread following behind it in a pattern that hung in front of my face, defying gravity. There was some kind of pattern there, but I had no idea what it was.

The Seamstress, however, was a different matter. She tapped her chin as she studied the thread's design, her eyes bright and considering. She looked like she was having a scholarly discussion and was very interested in whatever the other party had to say. She was even muttering to herself every now and again. "Yes, yes," and "Ah, I see," slipped from her lips.

I shot Lachlan a glance, and he was as entranced as I was. I'd never seen this type of magic before. Didn't even know what to call it.

Finally, the needle dropped out of the air. The floating thread unraveled until it hung limp. Just a normal thread and needle now.

The Seamstress bent and picked it up, then got back to work, sewing the rest of the jacket together. I waited for her to mention what the thread had said to her, but she stayed silent.

I caught her gaze. "Well?"

"A moment, just a moment." She finished the jacket, snipping the last thread and handing the needle off to the rat who had carried the little leather folder. She stepped back and dusted her hands together, then pointed to the long mirror on the other side of the room. "Well, go look at it."

I had to admit that I was a bit excited to see it, and I hurried off the stool. I wanted to know what the Seamstress had seen in the thread, but I also wanted to see the magic jacket that she'd created. I didn't know what it could do, but it clearly wasn't normal.

I stepped in front of the mirror and grinned. *Hey, not bad.* The jacket was made of a strong, dark gray fabric that looked fabulous in the short, slim-fitting style that the Seamstress had created. Occasionally, it looked dark as pitch, but from other angles, it shimmered with a dark gray sheen.

"What does it do?" I asked.

The Seamstress chuckled. "I have no idea. Something, definitely, but that depends on you."

"I get to choose?"

"Not precisely. The jacket will decide how you need it."

"Thank you." I didn't fully understand my new piece of outerwear, but I knew it was special. "What do I owe you?"

"Nothing. This was a favor. I would have quoted you a price if you would owe me."

"Thank you double, then." I smiled. "But what did the thread say?"

"Ah, yes. The thread. It told me that you seek the Corryvreckan whirlpool." Her eyes turned dark. "I'd like to advise you against that."

"We have no choice," I said.

Lachlan stepped forward. "Many of our friends are at great risk if we do not find the whirlpool."

The Seamstress sighed. "Yes, I can imagine so. No one ever comes here on a lark."

"Can you tell us how to get there, then?"

She nodded. "You'll need a boat and a guide. You can find those down at the docks. A Pike demon named Fearnan will help you. He's a fisherman whose boat is berthed near the far west end."

"Do we tell him that you sent us?" Lachlan asked.

"Yes, though he'll still demand a heavy price. The journey is dangerous. Deadly, in many cases. He'll have to take your mettle and determine if you're able to make it across."

"We are." Determination sounded in my voice, strong and fierce.

The Seamstress smiled. "I think you might be. And best of luck to you. I believe you will need it."

"I always need it." I tugged at the hem of the jacket. "Thank you again."

"Wear it well."

I gave her my old jacket in exchange for the new, and we left, turning right out of the shop as she'd advised us. The road slanted slightly downward, toward the water. I could smell it, the scent growing stronger as we neared.

A moment later, Muffin appeared at my side. *Nice new threads.*

At the mention of thread, I grinned. "You have no idea."

Lachlan glanced at me. "Talking to Muffin?"

"Yep."

Are we going to get dinner?

"No. Why do you ask?"

Smells like dinner.

"It smells like old fish. Ah, right. Of course. It smells like dinner. Don't steal anything."

Steal? Me? Never.

I laughed as we walked between a couple of old, ramshackle warehouses and stepped onto the wharf. There were a dozen rickety wooden docks jutting out into the sea. A boat was tied off to each, though they were unlike any boats I'd ever seen. For one, they were as creepy as the buildings we'd left. For another, they had faces.

Well, most of them, at least. Garish faces were painted onto many of the boats, their mouths gaping and filled with fangs. One of the boats looked like it was draped in old seaweed, a shipwreck raised to the surface to ride the waves once again. There was a legit pirate ship at the far east end, its mast hanging with ragged black sails and a plank jutting off the side.

Honestly, I wanted to ride that thing to the whirlpool, but we were meant to go to the west side and seek out Fearnan.

As if he knew where we were going, Muffin turned left and headed down the wharf to the east end, trotting quickly along, his little wings quivering with excitement.

"How do you know where we're going?" I asked.

Don't. I just smell dinner.

At the end of the docks, we found a demon standing with his back to us, working on something at a waist-high table. As I neared, I realized that he was cleaning a fish, his knife blade flying as he chopped it up.

Muffin jumped onto the table next to him, standing inches from the fish. *Hey, good buddy. Whatcha doin?*

Trust Muffin to make friends with a demon in return for fish.

"Hello, cat," the demon growled.

He didn't answer Muffin's question, so I assumed he couldn't understand him like I could. He handed Muffin a piece of fish anyway, which the cat took with a rumbly purr.

Maybe this demon wasn't so bad after all.

He turned to us, his pale green horns glinting in the light. A ferocious scowl creased his ugly face. "What the hell are you looking at?"

Okay, maybe he was only nice to cats. I couldn't blame him, though. People sometimes sucked, and cats never did.

I held up my hands in a placating gesture. "We're looking for help getting to the whirlpool."

He laughed. "You got a death wish?"

"I'm dead if I don't get there, so I wouldn't call it a death wish. More like an imperative."

"Fancy words." His scowl deepened. "It'll cost you. And you'll probably die."

"Like I said, I'm dead if I don't go, so *probably* isn't going to scare me."

"We can pay," Lachlan said. "If you can take us."

"Twenty thousand pounds, then," Fearnan said.

"What?" I nearly screeched the words.

"Like I said, you'll probably die. I'd probably die if it weren't for these." He tapped the side of his neck, and I realized there were gills there. His hands were webbed, too. "There are enough dangers out there that my boat will probably sink. I'll survive because I can swim back, but I'll need a new boat. Hence, twenty thousand pounds."

I glanced at Lachlan, then back at Fearnan. "So we're buying you a new boat."

"A replacement boat," he corrected. "But if it doesn't sink, then yes, a new boat. You want to get there or not?"

"We want to get there." Was this guy really our only hope? That was *so* much money.

But the docks were empty. Despite the dusky color of the sky, it was daylight here. There should be sailors and fishermen here, but there weren't.

Just Fearnan.

Our only option.

And we didn't have a choice. I probably shouldn't have led

with the "I'm dead if we don't go" bit. It might have made him raise his price. We were desperate, and he knew it.

Lachlan was already pulling his wallet from his pocket. "Do you take card?"

"What does this look like, a shopping mall?"

It sounded weird to hear a demon say shopping mall. The way he pronounced the words suggested that he'd only ever heard of such things, never seen them. Which made sense, given the fact that he had gills. He'd stand out like a sore thumb in a mall.

"We don't have twenty thousand in cash," Lachlan said.

"You don't need it. I know who you are. You stink of the Protectorate."

"How can you tell?" I asked. "And how does that help us?"

"They pay their debts. I'll collect from them if you die. If you don't die, I'll collect from you when this is all over." He laughed, as if the idea of us not dying were absurd.

"Okay, then." I nodded. "Let's go."

4

Fearnan was totally convinced that we would die, and as soon as his rickety wooden boat pushed away from the dock, I was pretty sure he was right.

The boat had to be almost one hundred years old, at least. The old fishing boat was about forty feet long with a flat deck. A closed-in wheelhouse would protect the captain from the elements, and the bow was planked in rough wood and looked almost worn through in places.

Muffin stood on the dock, watching us cast off. *I'll come join you if you need me.*

"Don't want to ride along?"

His green gaze traced over the boat's lines, skepticism flashing within. *I don't have a death wish.*

I did, apparently. I waved goodbye to Muffin, then turned to Fearnan, who stood inside the wheelhouse.

The door was propped open, and he turned back to me. "You go to the bow. Watch for dangers."

"Anything I should look for?"

Fearnan grinned, revealing a mouthful of pointed fangs. "Everything."

"All right, then." I joined Lachlan on the bow, standing with my feet braced as the waves rolled the boat around.

The sharp, salty air blew my hair back from my face as I stared out at the gray sea. Whitecaps topped the silvery waves, which stretched on for endless miles. Next to me, Lachlan stood, tall and strong, his arms crossed against his chest.

"You look like you were made for the sea," I said.

He looked at me and grinned, his hair swept back by the wind. "Aye?"

"Aye. A regular sea captain." But I meant it. It suited him.

"Hopefully I'll have a sea captain's eye." He turned back to the ocean, alert. "Because there's nothing good out there, and we need to spot it before it's too close."

He was right. I could feel the danger in the air. Not the prickle of dark magic or the stench of evil. Just plain old, regular danger that came when you rode a rickety old boat out into the North Sea while whitecaps crashed on the bow.

After a while, the sky in front of us began to darken. The clouds rolled toward each other, forming a dense black wall that started at the horizon and reached high into the air. Lightning cracked within the clouds, bolts so big that they lit up the dim sky, nearly blinding me.

Thunder rolled toward us a few seconds later, loud enough to make my ears hurt. "That's not a normal storm."

As if he agreed, Fearnan leaned out of the wheelhouse and shouted at us. "Bad news! We can't get through that storm."

I turned to face him. "We just started! We can't turn back now!"

"I'm just doing you a favor, lady! We go into that storm, and you die. That's the only thing that happens when a HellStorm comes at you."

Frustration beat in my chest as I turned back to the storm. My skin prickled with wariness and the black magic that echoed in the storm. It was closer now, black clouds roiling and lightning striking. The thunder came only two seconds later. Soon, it would be one second. The storm was bearing down on us faster than we were approaching it.

I turned back to Fearnan. "It's coming no matter what! Even if we try to outrun it, we won't make it!"

"We can try!" he shouted through the wind.

"I can control weather!" Lachlan's voice was loud enough to cut over the thunder.

"I have a bit of power, too," I shouted.

"Weather witches?" Fearnan asked.

"Sort of!" I said. I didn't know how much good I'd be able to do, but my gift over the environment had been growing. Hopefully I could help Lachlan. "We can minimize the storm. Keep going!"

"Your funeral!" Fearnan steered to boat into the storm.

A moment later, the wind began to whip ferociously, nearly driving me backward. I braced myself against it, trying to stay upright.

"We'll wait until we're almost in the center," Lachlan said. "Save our magic for the worst of it."

"Okay!" Something hit me in the back, and I jumped, then turned.

Two ropes lay at my feet. I looked up at Fearnan.

"Don't be an idiot! Tie off!"

It reminded me of the safety harnesses on the buggy.

As the wind buffeted us and rain began to pour, Lachlan and I each looped the ropes around our waists and secured them to a cleat near the bow.

When the waves began to grow, reaching fifteen feet in height, I looked at Lachlan. "I'm starting to think this wasn't a great idea."

"It was the only idea." Rain dripped off his face and hair, but his expression was determined.

And he was right. It was really our only option.

We stood, side by side and holding hands, then faced into the wind. I could barely see through the pouring rain, and every time the boat plunged down into the trough of a wave, my stomach pitched. The thunder was striking almost simultaneously with the lightning.

We were in the heart of the storm.

"Now!" Lachlan shouted.

His magic surged on the air, the scent of a forest so strange against the sea salt air. The wind howled slightly less, the thunder cracking less often. Still, the storm raged. Massive waves crashed against the bow, sending water rushing around our legs. I nearly lost my footing, but Lachlan clutched my hand.

I joined him, calling on the elemental magic within me, focusing on the water that surrounded us. I gave it everything I had, pushing my magic out into the waves, making them calm just before they reached us.

They were still massive, but my magic made them slightly smaller. I pushed more of my power toward the clouds. They were made of water, so maybe I could control them.

That was harder. While it was easy to get a grip on the ocean —it was so big it was hard to miss—getting a handle on the clouds was a hell of a lot more difficult. They kept slipping through my grasp, continuing to pour rain down upon us.

Lachlan was minimizing the thunder and lightning. It struck less frequently, but it still continued to shoot bolts into the sea. One blast hit so close that the thunder made me go temporarily deaf.

Lachlan shouted at me, but I could hear nothing.

Then the wave came. While I'd been trying to control the

clouds, I'd lost my hold on the waves. The huge wall of water plowed over the bow, knocking my legs out from under me.

Panic made my stomach drop. I slammed into the deck, the wall of water surging around me and tearing my hand from Lachlan's. The water stung my nose and eyes. I gasped, choking on seawater as I scrabbled on the deck, trying to get a hand on something.

I found nothing.

The wave washed me overboard. I plunged into the sea, the water closing around me, freezing cold and dark.

Fear iced my veins as my heart thundered. I kicked upward, reaching for the safety line that was still around my waist. The water tore at me as I tried to drag myself up the line. The boat was still moving, so the current hauled me backward, making the job ten times as difficult.

My lungs burned as I struggled to pull myself up the rope, fear making my limbs tremble. Finally, my head burst free of the ocean. Rain poured against my face as I gasped in air. The current at the side of the boat was fierce, nearly forcing me back under.

No way in hell I was going to let that happen.

My muscles ached as I pulled myself up the rope. I was halfway out of the water, reaching for the side of the boat when my line snapped.

I felt it give, so fast and abrupt that I couldn't even scream.

They never find you if you fall off.

I'd heard the boating fact somewhere, and in that moment, it blazed so intensely through my mind that I knew I was dead. If you fell off a boat in an ocean like this, you were dead.

I could control water, and maybe I could still save myself, but the thought echoed in my mind, strong and fierce.

I plummeted back toward the water, gravity pulling me

downward so that the sea could claim its prize. Desperate, I stretched my arm out, reaching for the boat.

But it was too late.

A strong hand grabbed my wrist, jerking me to a halt. Elation flared. I looked upward. Lachlan had my arm. He pulled, and I helped, scrambling up onto the boat. I tugged off the remains of the safety rope and threw it aside, then collapsed on the deck.

"Holy fates, you're a lifesaver," I said.

"Just a timesaver. You'd have gotten yourself out of that, but this was quicker."

"Better for my mental health, too." Maybe I could save myself from an enormous, angry, deadly ocean. But I didn't necessarily want to find out.

Still, the storm raged.

I stayed crouched on the deck, wedging myself against a piece of metal machinery to keep from going overboard again. Even if I still had a safety line, I clearly couldn't trust it.

"Together!" I shouted. "You take the sky. I'll take the sea!"

Our problem before had been that I'd tried to do both. Better to focus. Especially when a wave could capsize us.

"Aye!" Lachlan's magic surged, pouring out into the sky as he forced the clouds to calm, the lightning to fade.

I worked on the ocean, feeling the waves within me like they were part of my soul. I calmed the sea, pushing the waves down until they were manageable.

"Keep it up!" Fearnan shouted. "We're almost through!"

Rain and wind beat at us as the rickety old boat struggled through the sea, pushing ever onward as we tried to keep the storm at bay. The waves rolled at us, large enough to make my stomach pitch, but not so big that they would swamp the boat.

Finally, we made it through the worst of the storm. It took

less magic to control the water, until finally, we rolled on rocky waves of a normal, non-deadly height.

"Are you still controlling the weather?" I asked Lachlan, as a gentle rain pattered on my face.

"No." He lowered his hands. "Just stopped."

I sagged, my muscles going lax.

"We're through!" Fearnan shouted. "Not bad!"

I raised a brow at Lachlan. "High praise."

"Aye, he's full of compliments, that Fearnan."

The boat seemed to creak even more than it had before the storm, and I patted the deck gratefully. It had gotten us through.

The sky was a solid gray color, dreary and dull. For as far as I could see in any direction, the sea was empty. Just rolling waves, gray upon gray. Fearnan had to be using a compass or some other navigational system, since there were absolutely no landmarks by which to navigate.

"How far are we?" I shouted back to him.

"Hard to say. Depends on what the ocean throws at us."

"So there will be more," I muttered.

Lachlan's expression turned grim. "Aye, but we'll handle it."

The boat continued to rock onward, the old motor pushing us toward our destination. I kept my eyes on the horizon, hoping it would keep the sea sickness at bay.

I'd nearly been lulled into a trance by the time something thumped hard against the hull.

I jumped. "What's that?"

Fearnan darted out of the wheelhouse and leaned over the side of the boat, looking down. At first, he was silent. Then there was another thump, louder than the last, and so hard that it shook my bones. The whole boat shuddered.

"Fates alive, it's the Weeden." Fearnan's voice trembled.

"What's the Weeden?" Lachlan asked.

A massive green tentacle reached up from the depths and

wrapped around the bow of the boat.

"That," Fearnan said. "And if we don't cut it off at the source, it'll drag the boat down."

My heart leapt into my throat as the tentacle tightened around the bow. Only then did I realize that it wasn't a tentacle at all. It was a massive sea vine. Plant, not animal.

"We have to cut it from below?" I asked as I hurried to the edge of the deck.

"There's a main stalk, about forty feet down. Give or take twenty feet," Fearnan said. "The vines that shoot off of it wrap around the boat. Cut the main one, and they'll all go."

"Right, then." I looked at Lachlan, who'd joined me at the side of the boat. He nodded, unclipped his safety line, then drew his sword from the ether. I did the same, calling upon a large dagger.

I jumped overboard and plunged deep into the ocean. Cold water closed around me, a second shock to the system. I opened my eyes to the darkness and shook my hand, igniting the magic in my lightstone ring. It glowed, illuminating the dark water around me.

My eyes burned from the salt and my vision was weird, but I spotted the vines wrapped around the hull of the boat. They came up from the depths, tapering toward a central point deeper in the water. I kicked toward them, driving myself deeper as the cold water surged around me.

I could feel the water like it was part of myself, and though my lungs ached from lack of air, it wasn't as bad as it could have been. My water power was helping me.

Lachlan appeared out of the corner of my vision, swimming down as fast as he could. He was bigger and stronger than me, moving powerfully through the water. I kicked harder to keep up, following the vines down. They grew closer together as they neared their central stalk.

Icy cold made my limbs awkward as I struggled to go deeper. Forty feet, my arse. This was sixty or seventy, at least.

Finally, we reached the central point where a massive stalk grew up from the depths of the ocean. The smaller vines grew out of it, reaching up toward the boat that floated on the surface.

I prayed we weren't too late as I reached the huge stalk of seaweed and began to saw at it with my dagger. Lachlan joined me, cutting at it from the opposite side.

My lungs and muscles burned as I worked, but slowly, the blade cut through the weed. I couldn't imagine how badly Lachlan wanted to breathe. He didn't have my power, after all.

Finally, we severed the stalk. I kicked away from it, moving to swim upward.

Horror swept through me when I realized I had no idea which way was up. The sky was so dark from above that the water didn't glow from the surface. Everything was a uniform black outside of the glow of my lightstone ring. I looked all around for the stalk that we had severed, hoping to find it to orient myself, but it was gone.

My heart thundered as I kicked, trying to figure out which way to go. Close by, Lachlan seemed to be having the same problem.

I was about to call on my water magic, though I had no idea how it could help me here, when an idea flared.

Carefully, I released some of the air in my lungs. The bubbles spilled forth, rising.

I followed them, kicking for the surface, every muscle burning. Lachlan did the same.

We had only risen a few yards when something huge appeared overhead.

The vines!

Now that they were disconnected from their source, they'd died and lost their grip on the boat above. They sank through the water, heavy and huge, almost like a massive spiderweb falling down through the water.

I tried to kick away, to escape them, but a huge one hit me on the head, forcing me deeper into the water. I struggled and flailed but couldn't make any progress. We were so deep that the ocean felt like it weighed a million pounds. Like we were swimming through pudding while trying to dodge huge falling objects.

It was impossible.

Unable to help myself, I screamed, bubbles flaring toward the surface. The vine continued to force me deeper. Frantic, I tried to kick away from the vine, but it was big and heavy.

My muscles felt frozen with fear as I struggled. Out of the corner of my eye, I saw that Lachlan was trapped under another vine. He swam out from under it but was hit by another.

They were falling like logs through the water, and it was impossible to escape them.

I did the only thing I could—I called on the water to help us. With every ounce of magic and strength, I commanded the water to force us upward.

It did, at first. But it also forced the vines up. They were so damned heavy that it was more than I could manage.

My lungs burned so badly that I almost sucked in water. To my right, Lachlan's body went limp. Without my water power, he'd run out of breath.

No!

Terror like I'd never known surged through me.

He couldn't be dead!

We floated amongst the huge dead vines as the water tried to force us upward. I used every bit of power I had, begging the sea to help us. To get us to the surface.

Please.

5

Something wrapped tight around my wrist, and I startled, looking over.

A woman had grabbed me. No, a mermaid. Her hair was made of weeds and her eyes glowed an eerie green. Frilly gills decorated her neck, looking almost like a necklace, and her tail fin was at least eight feet long.

I pointed to Lachlan and screamed, "Save him, too!"

Bubbles poured from my mouth and my words were unintelligible, but she seemed to understand. She dragged me toward him, dodging the huge vines with such swift skill that I could barely comprehend it.

She grabbed Lachlan's wrist and raced for the surface, dragging us with her. Water rushed by me, along with the dead vines that continued to sink toward the seafloor.

We broke through the surface of the ocean, and I gasped, desperately sucking in air as I reached for Lachlan's limp body.

"Your boat is there!" The mermaid pointed behind me, her voice sounded bubbly and weird.

I turned, catching sight of it fifty yards away. Too far for me to drag Lachlan's body and have any hope of getting the water out of his lungs in time.

Desperate, I turned back to the mermaid, catching her green eyes. "Can you take us?"

Before the words had fully left my mouth, she'd grabbed our arms again and started to drag us. We were at the boat seconds later. Fearnan leaned over the side.

"Help me get him up!" I screamed as I climbed onto the boat. I was still lightheaded from lack of air, my water power only able to help me so much.

Fearnan grabbed Lachlan as the mermaid helped push, and his limp body thudded onto the deck.

His skin was pale and his eyes closed. I scrambled over to him, fear icing my skin.

"Lachlan!" I slapped him, but he didn't wake.

Water in the lungs.

I debated CPR, but that almost never worked. Instead, I placed my hands on his chest and called upon my magic, feeding my healing light into him. My palms glowed and so did his chest, lighting up with the healing power that Sulis had given me.

The light of life, she'd called it.

Well, it'd better work.

Hot tears poured down my face as I tried to bring him back. Panic made my heart thunder. I didn't want to imagine a world without Lachlan. Especially if he died trying to save my sorry ass.

"Come on, damn you!" My voice broke.

Finally—freaking finally—he coughed up some water. Then some more.

"Breathe!" I cried.

He did, sucking in a ragged breath as his eyes popped open. They went straight to mine, their dark depths pinned to me.

I loved him.

The thought flashed so suddenly through my mind.

I'd almost lost him, and it had made me realize that I loved him.

It had been a crazy short time, but it was true. Nearly losing him made it so obvious.

I was about to blurt it out when he sat up.

"Holy fates, that was close." He scrubbed a hand over his face. "What happened?"

I threw my arms around him and squeezed, a near-hysterical laugh bubbling up. "A mermaid saved us."

I let go of him, giving him one last desperate look, then turned to look over the side of the boat.

The mermaid floated there, her green eyes on us. All of her was green, actually. A pale, gray-green that looked like the sea at dusk. She looked like a cross between a fish and a person, with more fishy attributes to her top half than I was used to seeing in fictional depictions of mermaids.

"Thank you," I said. "You saved us."

"I heard you calling for help." Her voice still bubbled, like she wasn't used to talking out of the water. "I've never heard that before."

"I have some weird magic." I didn't know quite how to describe it. There was the elemental magic that allowed me to control water, yes. But there was also the light of life and the understanding of my environment. Somehow, that had all combined to send out a signal that we needed help.

Thank fates for that.

"What's your name?" I asked.

"Merodia. I live near here, with my people."

"Never seen no mermaids before," Fearnan muttered.

I glared, not wanting his rudeness to drive our helper away. "Well, thank you. We owe you our lives."

"Don't get ahead of yourself," Fearnan said.

"What does that mean?"

He pointed to the bow, and I turned to look. It was tilted unnaturally low in the water, pointing down toward the sea.

"Oh, shit." I scrambled backward. We were sinking. In all the stress, I hadn't realized.

"The vines tore away some of the planks at the bow," Fearnan said. "We'll only float for another ten minutes or so. Fifteen, maybe."

Lachlan surged to his feet. "We can't patch it?"

"Don't have the materials. The planks and nails fell overboard when the vines tore away."

Shit, we had been too late. Frantic, my mind raced. We needed a boat. We had to keep going.

"I can help," Merodia said.

I leaned over the side of the boat. "Really?"

"I will go look for the missing planks and nails."

I stared at her, dumbfounded. "But they could be anywhere for miles, carried by the current as they sank."

"I can feel everything in my sea. Everything that is out of place, everything new that shouldn't be here. Give me five minutes."

"I'm afraid that's all we can spare." I glanced toward the bow. "Thank you."

"I'll be back."

She dived under the water. I turned back to Fearnan and Lachlan.

"Do you really think this will work?" Fearnan asked.

"Do you have any better ideas?"

"I was just going to swim home." He shrugged.

"And leave us to drown."

He shrugged again. "I explained the dangers."

He hadn't been exaggerating. But I couldn't think about a

scenario in which Merodia failed. We had to fix this boat. "Just assume she'll find the pieces. Do you have a hammer?"

"A mallet, yes."

"Well, get it, then."

He grumbled and turned, going back to the wheelhouse. My heart thundered as we waited, the bow dipping lower in the water. If I focused, I thought I could hear the water rushing in below deck.

Lachlan squeezed my hand. "We'll manage."

Tension thrummed in the air as I watched the sea, praying to see Merodia's green head popping up above the waves. I imagined her deep below the surface, seeking out the pieces we needed to put the boat back together. Her power had to be a bit like mine, sensing things in the environment around her.

Minutes ticked by as we waited. We were so low in the water that it was nearly to my shoes when her head finally popped to the surface. Four more mermaids were with her, all of them looking vaguely similar.

She held up some planks and grinned, revealing a mouthful of fangs. "I think we've found what you need!"

"We'll need to prop the boat up," one of the mermaids said. He was a guy, from what I could tell. "Then you can hammer the planks back in place."

The four mermaids gathered around the boat and put their hands to the hull. Then the sea rippled around them as their fins worked underwater. Slowly, the boat rose. Water poured out of the hole in the hull.

"Quickly!" grunted one of the mermaids.

I looked at Lachlan. "I'll hang over and do the repairs if you'll hold on to my legs."

He nodded. I took the hammer from Fearnan and ran to the bow, hanging over the edge. Merodia swam up, her arms full of wood and leafy seaweed. A smaller mermaid popped up next to her, holding a handful of nails. Some looked really old and rusty —maybe not even from this boat—but they'd have to do.

"I'll hold the planks and you nail," Merodia said.

Around us, the mermaids breathed heavily as they kept the boat floating high on the water. Most of the water that had flooded the hull had poured out, thank fates.

Merodia shoved some of the leafy seaweed against the gap and then put the board in place. "The weeds will close the spaces between the wood. Like the caulking I have seen on other boats." She smiled. "I've made a point to study the boats."

"Good thinking." I took a nail from the smaller mermaid and began to hammer the plank into place.

"It won't work well, or for long, though. Best get where you are going quickly."

The blood rushed to my head as I worked, but finally, the hole was patched.

Merodia swam back a few feet and inspected the repairs. "This is truly a terrible boat."

I laughed.

"Hey!" Fearnan sounded insulted. "It's floating, isn't it?"

"Indeed, it is," I said, trying to placate him. The last thing we needed was a pissed-off captain.

Slowly, the four mermaids swam away from the boat, letting it rest more naturally in the water. It floated at normal level, and I grinned. "Thank you. You saved us."

Merodia saluted. "Where are you going?"

"To the Corryvreckan whirlpool."

She grimaced, and the mermaids around her mimicked the motion. "Are you sure you want to go there?"

"We don't have a choice."

"No, I suppose you don't, if you're desperate enough to cross this sea."

"Any advice?" I asked.

"Don't try to hold on," she said. "You can't. Just let it take you."

"Sounds like fun." Lachlan's tone was deadpan.

A dire chuckle escaped me. "Anything else?"

"When you reach the other end, be worthy," she said.

"Be worthy?"

"You'll figure it out." She waved. "We must go now. The air isn't good for us."

"Thank you again!" I waved, but she was already gone, disappearing below the surface.

Her friends departed, too, and the sea lay quiet.

"I must say, you're handling this better than I expected," Fearnan said.

"We're not there yet," Lachlan said.

"True enough." He turned to head back to the wheelhouse. "Let's get moving. That seaweed caulking won't hold for long, and I'd like to get this old girl back to port."

I was tempted to explain to him that boats were things, not women, nautical tradition be damned, but I shut my mouth. He cranked the engine, and we powered on.

Exhausted, I flopped onto the deck, staring out over the bow.

Lachlan joined me. "Thank you for saving me."

I glanced at him. "Any time."

The memory of him, nearly dead, sent a renewed streak of terror through me. *I loved him.*

Should I tell him?

I glanced back at Fearnan, who was probably eavesdropping. Yeah, now was not the time. Especially if Lachlan said something terrible in return, like "thanks."

Yeah, better to hold on to that tidbit.

The boat cut through the waves, quickly making time toward the whirlpool. I prayed we were almost there. I was running out of strength and magic. Whatever the sea decided to send at us, it tended to be big. I didn't think I could handle much more.

I fell into a bit of a stupor, staring at the iron-gray sea in front of us. When a popping noise sounded behind me, I jumped.

I turned. "What was that?"

Fearnan looked up through the wheelhouse window, his face pale. "The compass just burst."

"Oh, shit." I scrambled upright, Lachlan following. "How does that happen?"

"Bad luck."

"You don't do maintenance?" Lachlan asked.

Fearnan looked at the boat around us. "Does it look like I do maintenance?"

"No."

"What does this mean?" I asked.

"We're lost." He shrugged. "Or at least, we will be. I can keep us going in this direction for a while, but eventually we'll veer off course. And there are no landmarks."

I looked up at the sky. It was such a uniform iron gray that it was impossible to see even a glimmer of the glowing sun. No way to tell east or west. Nothing in the ocean to give us any clues. And certainly no stars. Even if it were the right time of day, they'd be hidden behind clouds.

Not that I knew how to use a sextant, anyway.

I looked back at Fearnan. "Did you really think we'd make it to the whirlpool?"

"No." Honesty sounded in his voice. "Definitely not. That's why I charged you so much."

Understanding dawned, followed by the memory of what Merodia had said about the whirlpool. "And if we did make it, were you going to take us through the whirlpool?"

Could we even make it without a boat?

"No. I never thought we'd make it." He didn't even look a

little bit remorseful. "The boat was supposed to sink, then I was going to take the compass and swim back."

"You can't tell direction in the water?" I asked.

"I'm a Pike demon, not a damned fish. I can swim well, but not find my way across hundreds of miles of open ocean."

"And you don't have a spare compass." I grinned. "Well, it looks like we're in this pickle together."

"It looks like we're all dead," Fearnan grumbled.

"This is hardly close to dead." I looked at Lachlan. "Right?"

"Aye, it's nothing."

"Lost at sea?" Fearnan thundered. "Floating on a rickety old tub?"

"Well, you're the one who didn't check his equipment, so I hardly think you should be complaining." I grinned. "I'll find a way to get us to the whirlpool, and you'll take us through it. Not only will that allow you to honor the original bargain, you can find a new compass there and get home."

Fearnan's expression turned thunderous.

"That's your best offer," I said. "And you'll make it back so you can get paid! Even better."

"Fine," he grumbled. "But how are you going to find the whirlpool?"

I turned to the bow, hoping my plan would work. "Just like the mermaid finds things."

I lay down on the edge of the deck on my stomach, then hung my hand in the water. The cold bit at my fingertips, but it worked. I could feel the ocean even more strongly now. Just like I'd been able to feel the fresh dark dirt in the desert.

I closed my eyes and focused, calling on my magic.

"Want some help?" Lachlan asked.

I blinked. "Yes, actually. Good idea."

I was running through my magic quickly here, and this was a

delicate operation. There was no telling how far the whirlpool was.

Lachlan sat next to me, laying a hand on my shoulder. He fed his power into me, just like he had back in the cottage where Hansel and Gretel had taken care of the witch. Back then, it'd been an attempt to help me learn how to access my magic. Now, it was a partnership. The two of us putting our magic together and making something bigger and stronger.

It was easier to feel the sea now, as if my reach extended out farther. Lachlan was like a magical battery, and boy, was I feeling the power.

In the distance, several miles ahead and slightly to the left, I felt a disturbance in the ocean. It was a massive amount of energy, swirling around and around.

"I've found it!" I pointed my free arm in the direction of the whirlpool. "Go that way."

"Weirdest compass I ever saw," Fearnan muttered.

His footsteps thundered back toward the wheelhouse, and the engine rumbled to life. The current dragged at my hand as we powered forward, but I kept it submerged, making sure that we were on track. It took a few adjustments in our direction, but eventually, Fearnan's shout sounded over the engine.

"It's ahead!"

I stood, my skin freezing from the cold wind that whipped across my wet clothes. Up ahead, a massive whirlpool spun in the middle of the ocean.

Fear chilled me even more.

"We have it on good authority that this thing is actually a portal. But damn if it doesn't look scary." Everything in my body screamed to get away. A whirlpool like that was the stuff of nightmares.

"It'll be okay." Lachlan squeezed my arm. "We trust Mordaca and Aerdeca."

And that was the heart of it. We did trust them.

Enough to jump into a deadly whirlpool, apparently. I turned back to Fearnan. "Drive straight for it."

"I know," he grumbled.

I grinned cheekily at him, but it didn't make me any less afraid. I gripped Lachlan's hand tighter and turned back to the whirlpool. It grew closer and closer. With every yard, my heart thundered louder.

I ignited the magic in my lightstone ring, knowing that it was probably a bad idea. Did I really want to see what was in the darkness of the whirlpool?

Hell yeah.

It was the size of a football field, roaring as it swirled round and round, ready to suck us into the depths of the sea. If this went wrong, even my water power wouldn't get us out of it. Merodia and the mermaids couldn't save us.

We'd be dead.

It was my last thought as the bow of the boat tipped into the roaring water, and the freezing liquid devoured us whole.

6

Darkness closed around me as the whirlpool sucked us in. My ring glowed faintly, shining on thousands of bubbles that swirled around us. I clung to the rail of the boat with my right hand and to Lachlan with my left, but the cold force of the water was too strong.

I lost my grip on the rail, and the boat disappeared from beneath my feet. I clung to Lachlan, refusing to let go. No matter what happened down here, we'd do it together.

The water tore at us as we spun round and round. Briefly, I caught sight of the boat. Then of Fearnan, swirling down with us. My lungs began to burn as we went deeper. Worry for Lachlan flared.

Then we were sucked into the portal. The ether grabbed hold of us and flung us through space. I lost all track of time and place. I couldn't even tell if I was spinning anymore, or if there was water around me.

But I could feel Lachlan's hand. I clung tightly to him, desperate not to let go. We had to stay together.

Finally, the ether thrust us upward, and my head broke

through the surface of the water. Gasping, I blinked and looked around, searching for the boat.

It bobbed upright, looking like it'd been ejected from a watery burial. The wood was ragged and gray, the wheelhouse missing its glass, and the motor sat askew.

"That thing looks like it should have stayed on the bottom of the sea," Lachlan said.

"I can't believe we rode it across open ocean."

"Hey!" Fearnan shouted. "She's a faithful friend."

"It," I muttered. "*It* is a faithful friend.

"What?" he demanded.

"Nothing!" I let go of Lachlan's hand and swam for the boat, cutting quickly through the water.

We scrambled onto the deck. Panting, I straightened and turned around. My gaze caught on a bright green island in the distance. It rose out of the sea, mountains sloping upward toward the sky. Stone buildings dotted the edge of the island, and it looked like a huge wall surrounded the perimeter.

"I think we're here," I said.

"Not very inviting," Lachlan said.

"They made us ride a deadly whirlpool just to get here." I grinned. "I don't think they're the welcoming type."

Fearnan sighed. "They're not."

"And you hadn't intended to come at all." I clapped him on the shoulder. "But now, here you are! Best of luck."

He glowered at me, then went to the wheelhouse and cranked on the engine. It rumbled to life, and the boat powered forward.

As we neared the island, I realized that the gray walls that surrounded it were higher than I'd expected.

"Looks like the only entrance is through that gate." Lachlan pointed to it. "Hope they open it."

It was a huge stone thing with two great doors that descended straight into the water.

The boat slowed as it approached. I considered shouting at the gate, hoping that a guard would hear me and open the stone doors, but it was unnecessary. As if they sensed our presence, they began to swing open.

It was slow going, the doors pushing away tons of water as they opened.

"It's really not the best engineering for the water, is it?" I asked.

"It may be a show of strength," he said. "Though who's going to attack them, anyway, if they have to get through that whirlpool? We only made it because you have gifts that helped us."

"Good point." I didn't like pointless shows of power, and I had a feeling I wasn't going to like the people who'd built that gate.

Fearnan steered the boat through the opening. The water within the harbor was calm and placid. It stretched like a mirror across an expanse that was roughly the size of a football field. About a dozen boats were tied off to the docks, but it was the land behind that caught my eye.

Brilliantly green, it swept upward to the peak of a mountain. There was a single road leading up from the harbor, with gray buildings on either side. A massive gray tower sat at the end of the road, spearing toward the sky.

"I think I know where we're headed," I muttered.

"Definitely their seat of power."

Fearnan directed the boat toward an empty slip and pulled up alongside. He jumped off and tied the boat to the cleats, then looked up. "You've got twenty-four hours. If you're not back by then, I'm leaving you."

"Fair enough." I climbed off the boat onto the wooden dock,

then strode up toward the quay. Lachlan joined me, and I glanced up at him. "I suppose we just walk right in."

"Aye, it's our best bet."

The town was deadly silent as we walked slowly up the street. A glance behind showed Fearnan veering off toward some buildings near the waterfront, no doubt in search of a compass to replace the broken one on his boat.

Curtains twitched in the windows, but no one came out of their houses to see who the newcomers were. A sense of strange magic hovered over the place, neither good nor bad. Definitely uncomfortable, though.

I shivered and kept walking. My clothes had dried stiff against my skin, and the chill still hadn't left my bones. Worse, my magic was nearly depleted, and I was weak from hunger.

Really not the best way to approach an unknown power cable of great magic.

At the thought, my hand burned, reminding me why we were here.

Yep. No choice.

The tower loomed ever higher as we approached. The green mountain speared up into the iron-gray clouds, making it look even more threatening.

As we neared, the magic grew stronger, prickling more fiercely against my skin. There was no wall surrounding the tower, but then, there didn't need to be. Two massive wooden doors were decorated with iron filigree that twisted and turned over the surface. We were about twenty yards away when they began to slowly swing open.

A single figure stood within the frame of the door, gray robes sweeping the floor. The hood concealed the face, but nothing could hide the aura of power.

"You come seeking answers," the figure said.

"I do." I stepped forward, stopping right in front of the door.

"Then come." The figure gestured us onwards, and we followed.

I glanced at Lachlan, and he nodded. We joined the figure in the huge entry hall. It turned and swept away, so we followed.

"I will take you to a place to rest for the night," the figure said.

"Night?" Lachlan asked. "But the sun is shining."

"Our seasons are opposite of yours, and being so far north, it is, in fact, nearly midnight. Not only is everyone asleep, but you will need your strength when you meet with the Elders of the Indomidae."

I didn't hate the idea of regrouping, not when the magic that flowed through the air here was strong enough to make my knees buckle.

"Thank you," I said.

The figure merely nodded, then led us to a large room that appeared to be a sleeping chamber. The ceiling arched high overhead, paneled with golden wood that gleamed. A fire burned in a large hearth, and a massive bed sat along one wall. A large wooden tub sat in front of a fire.

"Freaking honeymoon suite," I muttered.

The figure turned to me. "What was that?"

"Nothing. It's beautiful."

He—I could only guess that it was a he; the voice was too nondescript—swept a hand toward a table that sat in front of a little couch. Magic sparked more strongly on the air, then a huge platter of food and a pitcher appeared.

"Refresh yourselves. In the morning, someone will come to collect you for your meeting with the Elders."

We said our thanks, and the figure departed.

I turned to Lachlan. "Weird place."

"Aye." He scrubbed a hand over his chin and looked around. "Very empty, too."

"It's midnight."

"Still, it almost echoes with the emptiness."

I nodded. He was right. My stomach grumbled, and I went to the platter of food. I didn't recognize a single thing, but I dug in anyway.

"It's delicious," I said. Maybe I should've been worried about our circumstances, but I was too tired, weak, and hungry. Worry wouldn't get me anywhere, but eating would make me feel better.

Lachlan joined me, and we plowed into the food. As I ate, exhaustion began to pull at me. I glanced at Lachlan, remembering the revelation on the boat.

I loved him.

Should I tell him?

I opened my mouth, then shut it.

Nerves got the better of me, and exhaustion. This wasn't the right moment.

Yeah, that was it. It was about the moment, not cowardice. Totally not cowardice.

Okay, maybe a little of that.

We finished eating and took turns in the bath. I appreciated the view of Lachlan's bare chest, I couldn't lie. By the time we crawled into bed, my muscles felt like jelly.

I snuggled up against him.

This feels like home.

He leaned down and kissed my head, and warmth spread through me. This was real. Not just infatuation and lust. Real.

I moved closer to him and let sleep take me.

WHEN THE KNOCK sounded at the door the next morning, I jumped. My gaze moved to Lachlan. "Looks like it's time."

He nodded and rose, then opened the door to the same figure as last night.

Or was it?

Hard to tell, really. The cloak concealed anything distinguishable.

"You may come," the voice intoned. Power reverberated through the air, and I shivered.

We followed the figure out the door and down the wide corridor. It was done entirely in white, making me feel like I was approaching the pearly gates. I really hoped I wasn't.

"This place is weird as hell," Lachlan murmured.

"Ain't that the truth."

The corridor seemed to go on forever, and there wasn't a single window or piece of artwork in sight. The figure walked quietly in front of us, gray robes swishing behind him, his movement so smooth that it looked like he was floating.

Finally, we reached the end of the corridor. A massive room spread out before us, the ceiling so high that it disappeared inside some clouds.

"There are clouds *inside*." I whispered the obvious statement, but I was just so wowed that I couldn't help myself.

"Aye, it takes powerful magic to create that," Lachlan said.

In front of us, the floor turned to shimmering silver water. Flat stepping stones were laid out in front of us, leading across the gleaming surface.

The figure swept out a robed arm. "You must cross the stones to enter the sacred space, then you may speak with the Elders of the Indomidae. *If* you make it across."

There was always an *if*, wasn't there?

Lachlan stepped forward, determined to go first. Always throwing himself between me and danger, that man. I waffled between appreciation at the sweetness and annoyance.

"Be careful," I said.

"Aye, always." He looked back at me briefly, then stepped onto the first stone.

Then disappeared entirely.

Shocked worry pierced me. "What happened to him?"

"He is crossing." The figure gestured, sweeping his arm toward the stepping stones. "Now you must do the same."

I stepped forward immediately, determined to find Lachlan. Nothing happened at first, so I stepped onto the next rock, and the next.

The air around me began to shimmer, magic igniting.

Suddenly, I stood at the edge of a cliff, staring down into nothing. My stomach pitched and my head went woozy. I stepped back, breath caught in my throat.

"Oh, fates." I looked around. What the heck had happened?

The stepping stones had disappeared, and the ground was flat, boring dirt. Except for where it dropped off into nothingness.

"This is a test, isn't it?" I muttered.

Muffin appeared at my side, little wings fluttering to keep him aloft. *I bet you a pound of tuna that it is.*

"Yeah, definitely looks like a test." Bree's voice sounded from my other side, and I turned. She stood next to me, arms crossed and staring down at the cliff. "You're *not* going to like this."

Rowan appeared next to her. "She really isn't."

"What are you guys doing here?" I asked.

They looked up, almost surprised, then at each other.

"Shit, I don't know." Bree frowned. "We were in the vaults one minute, hunting more ingredients to make the potion that allows the tattooed Protectorate members to leave the castle, then I was here."

"I think we're here to help you. Emotional support on your test, and all that." Rowan reached out to touch me, and her hand passed right through. She grinned. "Yep. This is some cool magic. No idea how it's happening, but it's cool."

"Well, I'm glad you're here." It made me feel a bit calmer, just thinking about it. We'd had to split up in order to cover enough ground on the tattoo problem, but I preferred working with them. "How's it going, by the way?"

"Not bad," Bree said. "We've almost got our hands on enough potion to allow ten people to leave the castle for up to a week. That should help us hunt answers, or defend the castle if we ever need to."

"Good." I nodded. We were making progress. Slow, but I wasn't going to turn up my nose at any forward movement.

"You'd better get moving with your test," Bree said.

Muffin meowed. *Yep. Test waits for no one!*

"Freaking tests." I looked at Muffin, then at my sisters. "This is hero shit, that's what this is. Tests to prove my worthiness. What I'd do to achieve my goals. The hero's journey—the lot of it."

Better get climbing, then, eh?

Rowan grinned. "Suck it up, pal."

"It's so over the top." I cracked my knuckles, ready to get started with the horrible journey. Always heights, wasn't it?

With my heart pounding in my ears, I got down on my belly and looked over the edge of the cliff. Little handholds peeked out, jagged rocks and tiny indentions. It was enough that I could get down, but it wouldn't be fun.

"Here goes nothing." I shimmied off the edge, my skin feeling numb from fear.

My sisters followed, each taking up position on either side of me.

Slowly, I climbed down, my stomach doing jumping jacks. Muffin stayed by my side the whole time, shouting weird encouragement as I descended.

"You've got this," Bree shouted.

"It's a piece of pie!" Rowan said. "I prefer pie."

I laughed at her dumb joke, then regretted it when it made me lose my focus. I kept going, silent and determined. I never once looked down.

I spend far too much time encouraging you to climb great heights.

"I couldn't agree more."

"You talking to your cat?" Rowan asked. "We can't hear him, remember?"

"I am, but let me focus." Sisters!

My head was buzzing by the time I made it halfway. When I reached for a protruding rock that looked particularly promising, it broke off beneath my hand.

A tiny shriek escaped my throat as I hung there, scrabbling for another handhold. Muffin flew down and pressed his little paws against my butt, trying to keep me elevated.

Bree reached out and tried to grab my arm, but her hand passed right through since she wasn't really here.

"There's a handhold four inches higher!" Rowan shouted.

Heart thundering, I flailed until I grabbed the rock that she had pointed out and clung, my face pressed to the cliff as sweat chilled on my skin.

You got it? Muffin kept pushing hard on my butt, trying to keep me from falling.

"I got it." I panted, the words barely audible. My muscles trembled like jelly.

Muffin flew away, and I kept climbing down. By the time I reached the bottom, I was shaking.

Bree jumped down next to me. "Good work!"

"Not half bad," Rowan said.

"Thanks, guys." I turned from the cliff.

More stepping stones stretched out in front of me, creating a path through the silvery water. I turned back to the cliff, but it was gone. So were Rowan, Bree, and Muffin. My helpers had disappeared.

The huge white room with the cloud ceiling was back, and I was alone.

Annoyance flashed through me, a far better feeling than the fear. "Freaking tests."

I turned back to the stones and stomped across the water. Partway across, another gray-robed figure appeared. I stopped and waited.

"What would you do?" The figure's voice echoed with power.

"What do you mean?"

"What would you do?"

There were no clues in the figure's voice, but this was obviously another test of some sort. What would I do? To what? Achieve my goals?

What were my goals?

Save my friends. My family. Defeat the Fates to save the world.

"Anything." The word escaped my lips almost before I thought it.

The figure nodded and stepped aside, hovering over the water.

All right, then.

I continued on, stepping across the stones until I reached the other side.

When I reached it, the cloudy sky cleared. The path across the empty room was obvious, and I followed it to a massive archway. I stepped through into a huge round room with no ceiling. The sky above roiled with dark clouds. It poured rain and glinted with lightning. Through the open space above, I caught sight of a towering green mountain.

Beneath the open sky, the floor was a gleaming white marble. Though it was raining above, none of the water splashed on the floor below. In the middle, a green fire burned, reaching at least ten feet tall and seeming to flicker with images amongst the flames.

A dozen gray-cloaked figures sat around the fire, their faces obscured by their hoods. About twenty feet away, Lachlan appeared, stepping through an archway that was identical to the one I stood under. His face was pale and his gaze frantic as he searched the space.

When his eyes landed on me, they calmed. He rushed toward me, wrapping his arms around me. "Thank fates you're fine," he muttered into my hair.

Suddenly, I remembered what his greatest fear was. *Losing me.*

Was that the challenge he'd faced while crossing the stepping stones?

He pulled back. "At least we made it."

I nodded, but I could feel the gazes of the Elders upon us, so I turned to face them. I gripped Lachlan's hand. "Let's go."

7

We walked toward the Elders of the Indomidae and stopped at a gap in their circle that had clearly been left for us. The green flames died down until they were only three feet tall, short enough that I could see over them.

The Elders stood.

"You seek answers." They spoke as one, their voices echoing through the room.

"Um, yes." I couldn't figure out who to look at. I raised my hand. "My friends and I have been given these tattoos. They're imbued with a spell that will make us the slaves of the Roman Fates if we leave the protection of our castle."

"Let us tell you a story."

I blinked. "Wait, what?"

"Long ago, there was a seal that could turn into a woman." They spoke in unison still, not bothering to answer my question.

I glanced at Lachlan, who shrugged. So we listened, since there wasn't much else we could do. Now was not the time for being rude. Not when we needed their help so badly.

"This seal was one of many. In our land, it is believed that seals were once people who voluntarily gave their lives to the sea. Once a month, they are allowed to come upon the shore and shed their seal skins to take human form."

Where was this story going?

As if they heard my question, the Elders continued. "And thus, the seals climbed onto the shore on the thirteenth night of every month. They shed their skins and hid them away, and then began to dance and play games.

"One month, a farmer from the town of Mikladalur decided that he wanted to see if this were true. He went down to the shore and hid amongst the rocks. He waited, watching as the seals climbed upon the shore. One of the seals was a beautiful young woman, and as she lay her skin down upon the rocks, he watched her. After hiding her skin, she went onto the land to join the festivities.

"The party went on all night, and toward the end, the man crept from his hiding place and took the skin of the beautiful young woman. She returned to the place where she had hidden her seal skin and searched for it, to no avail. As she was crying, the farmer stepped from the bushes and showed her the skin. She begged for its return, but he would not relent. And thus, she was compelled to follow him toward his home."

The Elders paused in their story, just briefly. I frowned, really not liking where this was going. And I *really* didn't like this farmer.

"The man locked her seal skin away in the trunk, and wore the key tied around his neck at all times. The seal woman was forced to become his wife and bear him several children. No matter how much the seal woman wanted to return to the sea, she could not."

I scowled. What a kidnapping bastard that farmer was.

"One day while the man was at sea, he realized that he had left the key to the trunk at home. He turned to his fishing friends and said, 'Today I shall lose my wife.' The men rowed back to shore as quickly as they could, but by the time they arrived, the seal woman was gone. She had doused the fire and hidden the sharp knives so that the younger children could not hurt themselves. The farmer knew that she would not return."

Thank fates. It was about time the seal woman escaped.

The Elders continued with their story. "As for the seal woman, she ran to the ocean and put on her seal skin, then leapt into the sea. A large bull seal waited for her after all these years. She had loved him when she had first been abducted, and he had waited for her. She joined him once again in the sea."

Oh, I like the happy ending.

But the Elders were not finished. I frowned when they began to speak again.

"Any time the seal woman's human children went to the seashore, a seal would appear in the water, its head turned to look at the shore. The townspeople believed that this was the seal woman. And so the years passed. Until one day, when the men of Mikladalur planned to sail deep into the caverns along the sea and conduct a seal hunt. The seal woman appeared to her human husband in a dream and begged him not to kill the great bull seal that would be sleeping at the entrance of the cave, and to spare the lives of the two seal pups who were her children."

Oh no, this was not going to end well. Nerves skated across my skin as I waited for the Elders to continue.

"The men of Mikladalur began their seal hunt, and the farmer did not heed the message from the dream. He joined the others and killed the bull seal and the two young pups. For his own share, he took the head of the bull seal and the fins and flippers of the young seals. "

Oh, what a bastard. A total sociopath.

"Later that evening, after cooking the bodies that were the

seal family of his enslaved wife, a giant troll appeared in the farmer's cabin. Immediately, the farmer recognized the troll as his enslaved wife, transformed. She sniffed the food that was her family and shouted her curse: 'Here lies the head of my husband with his broad nostrils, the hand of Hárek, and the foot of Frederick! Now there shall be revenge, revenge on the men of Mikladalur, and some will die at sea, and others will fall from the mountaintops, until there be as many dead as can link hands all round the shores of the isle of Kalsoy!'"

I frowned. She was getting her revenge, and that was good in a sense. But it could in no way compensate for the loss of her family. And innocent people might die. The story opened a deep chasm of sadness within my chest, leaving me feeling empty for the seal woman and her late family. Even the people of Mikladalur.

The Elders continued. "Once the seal woman laid down her curse, she vanished and was never seen again. But today, her curse still lingers. The people of Mikladalur die in greater numbers due to tragedies at sea and falls from the cliffs. It is because of the selfishness of that one man, and his cruelty to the seal woman, that such horror remains."

Silence fell in the enormous room. I glanced at Lachlan, and his face was solemn.

"That's the saddest story I've ever heard." I blurted the words, realizing too late that they were out of place in the quiet room.

The Elders turned to me. "We agree."

"But what does it have to do with me?" How did this have anything to do with the tattoo and the curse that we bore? How would it help us save our friends?

"Does terrible have to stay terrible?" Once again, the words were said in unison.

"What do you mean?"

"Go." The word boomed through the huge room, every voice so loud that it shook my insides. "And do."

The world spun around me, and my head began to pound. Darkness crashed, and I fell to the ground. When I opened my eyes, all I could see were the stars above. Thousands of them glittering in the night against a blanket of inky black darkness.

Blinking, I sat up and looked around. The air was sharp and cold, and smelled of the sea and salt.

"We're not in Kansas anymore," I muttered. We were at the seaside. No, scratch that. *I* was at the seaside. Lachlan was nowhere to be found. I climbed to my feet and inspected my surroundings.

The waves crashed against the beach only fifty meters away, and large boulders had tumbled upon the sand. Enormous mountains rose tall behind me, and I'd guess that they were green in the daylight.

What the heck was going on? Was this a new test?

Moonlight glittered on the ocean waves, and I squinted at them, finally catching sight of tiny little lumps in the water. They moved closer to shore, eventually climbing upon the pebble beach.

Seals.

One by one, the seals crawled towards crevices in the rock and other hiding places. Beneath the light of the moon, they shifted into the form of humans and hid their seal skins among the boulders.

Understanding dawned.

I was witnessing the story of the seal woman.

I searched for the man who would steal the young woman's seal skin. What was I supposed to do if I found him?

I didn't know, but it had to be something. That story had been one of great injustice and tragedy, a story of one man's selfishness that had not only ruined the life of the seal woman, but also the lives of many of his fellow villagers.

I couldn't stand such selfishness and cruelty.

As quietly as I could, I crept over the rocks on the beach, hiding behind large boulders and hoping that the seal people would not smell or see me. Occasionally, I caught glimpses of the seals going toward the shore and dancing under the moonlight.

Wind swept my hair back from my face and cut through my clothes. Only my arms and chest were warm, protected by the jacket from the Seamstress.

Pebbles crunched underfoot as I walked. Finally I caught sight of a rustling in the bushes at the end of the beach. I approached, maintaining a low profile, and crouched behind. I squinted toward the bushes, sure that something was there.

A moment later, I spotted the man, hiding between the branches and peering out at the seal people. The glint in his eyes made me uncomfortable.

It was avarice, and I hated it.

I searched the shore, hoping to find the seal woman and warn her away from this area. But it was too late. She was already shedding her skin and standing up in the moonlight, just ten yards away.

Time seemed to race forward, like I was seeing the Elders' story in super speed. The young woman went up to the beach to join her friends, and the man stole her skin. She returned and they argued. She begged and cried, but he wouldn't relent.

My heart tore as I watched him begin the process of ruining her life. He would kidnap her and keep her for decades.

I couldn't let it happen.

"Crap." Indecision warred within me, but I couldn't watch this tragedy unfold. I began to creep out from behind the rock.

What's going on?

I stopped, turning back to see Muffin sitting on the boulder. His green eyes glinted in the moonlight, and his black wings looked semitransparent.

"I'm here to see. And do."

What the heck does that mean?

"I don't know, but I think it means I'm going to save that seal woman." That's what I wanted it to mean, at least.

You're going to change history? Haven't you seen the movies?

"You have a point." I frowned. "But it's just a story."

Then why do you care?

"Every story needs a happy ending." And I couldn't watch this happen, not if I could help the seal woman. I had to be here for a reason. *I had to.* It wasn't just to witness tragedy and do nothing.

That wasn't my style.

I stopped behind a rock, close enough that I could see the tears glinting on the seal woman's cheeks. My heart ached even as rage swelled within my chest.

I stared hard at them, trying to figure out the best way to stop this tragedy. As I stared, it felt like I could see something new. Particles in the air, almost like time had become a thing. A molecule.

What the heck?

Reach for it. Change it.

I didn't know where the voice came from. The Elders? I followed the command, acting on instinct.

Magic rose in my chest, strong and strange. *New magic.* I reached out with my power, using it to grab onto the molecules. To grasp time. I didn't know how I did it, and it barely made sense to me, but I could feel it. I knew what I was doing, somehow.

My magic wrapped around the molecules of time that seemed to float in the air, and I began to turn back time.

The world went silent. Even the waves ceased crashing.

Events began to rewind themselves, like a movie. The seal woman walked backward up the beach, returning to her revelry with the other partiers. Time creaked backward. The man laid down the seal skin and slipped back into the bushes. Eventually, the woman returned and donned her skin, then returned to the sea.

Enough.

Immediately, I heeded the voice and let go of my grip on time. I couldn't go back too far. It was too dangerous.

But now the events would replay, wouldn't they?

A moment later, a seal climbed onto the beach.

The seal woman.

As expected, she removed her skin and ran up the shore, having no idea what waited for her when she returned.

It didn't matter if I turned back time but didn't change anything. Everything was going to happen just as it had before, unless I stopped it.

I had to stop it.

The moonlight gleamed on the man as he snuck out of the bushes and moved toward the seal woman's skin. His movements were furtive, and the briefest flash of guilt seemed to race across his features.

Could I convince him to change his mind, if there were already a spark of guilt there? Probably not, since the seal woman's tears had done nothing, but I could try.

I crept toward him, moving quickly and silently amongst the rocks. He was almost to the skin when I jumped in front of him. "Don't do it. You'll regret it."

Shock flashed across his pale face, then his eyes hardened. "Who the hell are you?"

"It doesn't matter. But I know what you're going to do, and it's wrong. You can't kidnap her."

"Why? She's not even human." He shifted closer to the seal skin, his fingers twitching.

He's still going to do it.

Disgust bloomed within me. "You're a monster." I glanced up the beach to where the seal people were dancing under the moonlight. Their laughter echoed across the shore, joining the sound of crashing waves and creating a joyful symphony. "They look pretty human to me."

The man scowled, and I could see how much he didn't care. There was nothing but greed and desire in his eyes, and I was just in his way.

He moved toward the seal skin, inching a bit closer.

I shifted left, getting in his way. "I'll stop you." But I really didn't want to have to. I wanted him to make the decision for himself, though that seemed unlikely now. "I won't let you do this."

He gave me a look, his slimy gaze traveling up and down my body. "Maybe I'll make *you* my wife."

More disgust filled me. "That's not how this works. That's not how *any* of this works."

He's got a seriously skewed worldview. Muffin's voice sounded from behind, and I assumed he was hiding behind the rock.

The man drew a glinting silver knife. "Then I'll kill you."

"Is that how this works in your world? Wife or dead?" I scowled at him. "That's insane."

The annoyance on his face turned to rage, and he brandished his blade.

Annoyance flashed through me, and I drew my own sword from the ether. "Two can play at that game." I grinned. "And I *always* win."

He spat at my feet. "I don't like aggressive women."

"And I don't like slimy worm men." I grinned at my insult, delighted when he bellowed and charged me.

As the seal people danced behind us on the beach, oblivious to our battle, I collided with the man.

I didn't want to kill him, so I would have to be clever.

His blade flashed out, swiping for my middle. I sucked in, darting back just in time to avoid the blow. I kicked him in the stomach, sending him flying backward.

"You don't have to do this." I stood over him, my blade raised. "You can go meet a nice woman in the village and convince her to be your wife. You don't have to steal the life of the seal woman."

I could see in his eyes that my words did not register. He didn't want a normal woman from the village. He wanted to torture the seal woman by kidnapping her. She was just a thing to be owned by him.

No way in hell was I going to let that happen.

The man leapt to his feet and charged me, then swung his blade in a wide arc that sliced my arm. Or at least, it should have. He made contact, but the steel couldn't pierce my jacket.

Hell yeah. The Seamstress's gift was like armor.

"Didn't see that coming, did you?" I darted right, then swung my own sword, aiming for his leg.

He dodged just in time, and I questioned my desire not to kill him. I knew what he would do in the future, and it would be terrible. He would kill and destroy lives, and his selfishness would hurt future people in his village once the seal woman laid down her curse.

But still, I didn't want to kill him if I could help it. I didn't want to have too much effect on this story. But I was determined to save the seal woman.

Incoming! Muffin's voice sounded, saving me just in time as the man stabbed his blade toward my stomach.

I dodged, then attacked, swinging my blade as fast as I could toward his legs, but he was too quick.

He was a good fighter, the bastard.

We danced around each other on the beach, avoiding sword strikes. The moon provided enough light that I could see the blood lust in his eyes. I landed a blow to his thigh, and crimson welled. He returned the favor, delivering a thin slice to my calf. Pain flared, and I hissed.

The man lunged toward me again, his sword outstretched. His foot landed in the crevice between two rocks, and he fell, somehow going down on his blade in a way that sent the dagger driving through his heart.

I stumbled backward. "Holy fates."

It looks like you don't have to kill him after all. Muffin grinned, his fangs glinting in the moonlight. *And I say good riddance to bad rubbish.*

I sat on the rock, my lungs burning and heart speeding, and stared at the man's body. He twitched one last time and lay still. "Well, you were a bastard. I can't say that you didn't deserve it, nor that I'm disappointed I didn't have to deliver the blow."

It was a win-win, as far as I could see.

Muffin jumped up on the rock next to me. *You still changed history.*

"It's just a story." But still, I wondered if I'd done the right thing. Stories had purpose, after all. This one taught that you shouldn't abuse others.

But I was *here*. The seal woman was real, at least in this story realm. I couldn't watch her life go down the drain without helping.

And the man *had* killed himself, after all.

I looked toward the beach, where the seal people were dancing in the moonlight. Their laughter echoed across the shore, making something inside of me feel lighter.

I had to believe I'd done the right thing. *I had to.*

A moment later, the earth spun around me. Briefly, my

vision went black. When I opened my eyes, I was back in the enormous white room, sitting in front of the green fire and surrounded by the cloaked figures. Lachlan sat next to me, shock in his gaze.

I looked at him. "How long was I gone?"

"Only seconds."

"Felt like longer." I looked at the cloaked figures. "Did I do the right thing?"

"What did you learn?" The voices of the twelve Elders echoed in unison.

I sat back. What had I learned? I didn't care about that right now. "Did I do the right thing?"

"What did you learn?" The words boomed louder.

Okay, they were not going to answer *that* question. Apparently, that was for me to decide, or for history. Either way, I didn't regret saving the seal woman. I couldn't imagine the pain of years of captivity, or the agony of having my family killed. And then all the deaths that came after, once her curse had been laid down.

"I did the right thing."

"What did you learn?"

I sat back, my mind racing. What was this meant to tell me? And how did it relate to the tattoo? Understanding flared. "I can change fate." Holy crap. "I changed fate. Not just in stories, but in real life."

"One person's selfishness can change history." The voices boomed in the open space. "One person's goodness can do the same."

I wanted to fist pump. That meant I *had* done the right thing. Not just in *my* world, but in the real world.

The figures spoke again. "When you return to your realm, you must use this power wisely. You can alter the course of history, and that can cause great damage. Be wary."

I heard their warnings, but my mind raced with thoughts.

I could change fate.

Who changed fate in Celtic myth? Because that's where this power had to come from, right? And didn't this make me like an opposite side of the coin to the Fates?

I had the power that they no longer possessed.

It made me their perfect enemy.

No wonder I was fated to fight them.

The Elders stared at me, shaking me away from my questions.

Right now, I had to figure out how to save my friends. I raised my hand, showing them my tattoo. "I will be careful with this power. But how exactly does this help me save my friends? How does it help me get the tattoo off?"

"That tattoo is a component of the Doomsday Spell, one of the most dangerous pieces of magic ever created." Their voices deepened with seriousness.

I shivered. Freaking Doomsday Spell? "What is the Doomsday Spell?"

"The spell allows a group of powerful supernaturals to be enslaved. If the Fates control individuals as powerful as those at the Protectorate, they could use them to destroy the world and bring about Doomsday."

Horror welled in my chest. "That's evil." It was one thing to destroy the world. It was another thing entirely to use good people to destroy the world. *I* could be used to destroy the world? Hell no. "And it was stupid of you to create such a spell."

I shouldn't have said it, but I couldn't help myself.

Every one of the Elders of the Indomidae glared at me. I smiled weakly, not willing to take the words back.

The Elders glared again. "If you desire to stop the spell, you must locate the Doomsday Stone and destroy it. It is what the

Fates seek as well. They can use the stone to ignite the magic in the tattoo and make the enslavement curse invincible."

"Invincible?" Lachlan asked. "Do you mean that the Seawort protection potion won't be able to block the power of the tattoo if the Fates get the Doomsday Stone?"

The Elders answered him in unison. "Precisely. The stone is used in the last part of the spell, and it will make the enslavement permanent—no Seawort potion or other magic will be able to break the curse if the Fates obtain the Doomsday Stone. You will be enslaved for all days. The stone is so powerful that even a piece of it is enough to cast the Doomsday Spell."

Why did supernaturals create such powerful magic in single objects? It was so damned dangerous. "Do you know if the Fates have already found the stone?"

"They have not."

Okay, so we had to move fast to beat them to it. "What do I do once I get the stone?"

"You must destroy it and kill the Fates. Then the tattoos will be removed, and you will be free. But obtaining the stone will be difficult."

Of course it would be.

"Where is the stone?" Lachlan asked.

Their voices echoed as one, reverberating around the chamber. "You must go into the depths of hell. Into Dante's Inferno."

Oh, that was just perfect.

8

Fortunately, the Indomidae were able to send us straight back to the Protectorate castle. Since we didn't meet Fearnan within the twenty-four hour window he'd given us, I assumed he'd found a compass and returned to Demonville. Unfortunately, it meant walking into their green fire, which was also a portal. It had been *very* unpleasant, but fortunately brief.

"First things first, let's find Jude," I said as we crossed the castle lawn. It was strangely silent for a mid-morning.

"Aye." Lachlan nodded. "Then we eat."

My stomach grumbled, agreeing that it was a fabulous idea.

As soon as we stepped into the castle, I caught sight of Jude on the landing. Her starry blue eyes went straight to us. "Any luck?"

I nodded. "We'll update you. Want to go to the round room?"

She shook her head. "Kitchen. You look like you could use a meal."

It was like she'd read my mind. The Cats of Catastrophe hurtled down the stairs a moment later, as if they'd heard the word *meal*.

We all gathered around Hans's scarred wooden table in front of the fire, tucking into plates of sandwiches and boxes of juice.

"We're too busy for real meals these days, alas." Hans's mustache quivered with disappointment.

The cats didn't seem to mind digging into piles of sliced turkey, and I was certainly enjoying my sandwich. I told him so, but he just nodded and turned.

"The castle is under great strain," Jude said.

Lachlan polished off the last of his sandwich. "No surprise. But we'll get it settled. Soon."

Jude's gaze sharpened. "What did you learn?"

I told Jude all about the Doomsday Spell and the corresponding stone that was imbued with the magic to make the spell official.

"So, this whole time, the Fates have been seeking different pieces of a puzzle that will enslave the Protectorate," Jude said.

I nodded. "I think so. They got the first part of the spell from the Celtic Otherworld when they invaded my mother's village. They also needed power to fuel the curse, and I assume that's why they stole Arach's heart. They must have gotten enough from it to enact their plan." I could still remember the contraption they'd hooked the heart up to and the way power had dripped from the stone heart. We'd saved the heart, but not retrieved the liquid that had dripped from it. It must have been imbued with strong magic.

"They're getting the last part of the spell from the Doomsday Stone," Lachlan said. "We just have to stop them before they get it."

"Where is the stone?" Jude asked.

"The Indomidae said that we can find it in hell," I said. "Dante's Inferno, specifically."

Muffin's ears perked up. *Dante's Inferno? The nine levels of hell?*

"Yes. Why, do you know it?"

"What is your cat saying?" Jude asked.

I've spent time there. I know some shortcuts through the different levels, all the way to the bottom. We'll get there fast. Faster than the Fates.

Heck yeah. That would help. I turned to my human companions. "Muffin has spent time in Dante's Inferno." I'd have to make a point to ask him *why*. "He said he can lead us through the nine levels to get to the bottom, which is where the Indomidae said the stone would be encapsulated in ice."

"Why would the stone be in a hell that was explored by an Italian poet in the fourteenth century?" Jude asked.

"I don't know." I frowned. "Maybe because he is Italian and the Fates are from Italy? That's the only connection I could find."

"There's got to be something else," Lachlan said.

We'd have to figure it out. The Italian poet Dante Alighieri had written an epic poem about the hell so long ago. But it could be a useful guide for us since it explained the nine different levels of hell and all of the souls who inhabited it. But then, we also had Muffin.

Magic shimmered in the air, making the spot in front of the fireplace grow hazy. A moment later, Arach appeared, her semi-transparent form shimmering. Her somewhat reptilian features were strangely beautiful when viewed with the fire behind them.

"Did I hear you mention Dante Alighieri?" She drifted toward the table, interest glinting in her eyes.

I nodded. "Yes, what do you know of him?"

"He was an early member of the Protectorate, centuries ago."

"Really?" Jude's brows rose. "I had no idea."

"There have been so many members, I am not surprised you cannot recall all of them." She smiled. "I never met him during his tenure here—I spent much of those decades resting beneath the castle, regaining my strength from a battle in the previous century—but I do recall his name."

"Huh." I leaned back in my chair. "So it's possible he went to the Inferno on a mission for the Protectorate, then wrote about it."

"If he did, he never mentioned the mission in his book," Lachlan said.

"You've read it all?" I asked.

He nodded. "It was...odd. From another time."

"He was a strange one, from what I have heard," Arach said. "There were whispers. He was not right in the head. And not in a harmless way."

"I got the sense from his writing that he was very fascinated by the misery of hell," Lachlan said.

Definitely an odd duck, then. Muffin scowled, his lined face creasing even more. *Because that place is freaking miserable.*

"Should he have been at the Protectorate, then?" I asked.

"Perhaps not. But like I said, I was asleep for most of his life. I don't know any details. He may have been harmless."

"Well, we'll get started right away," I said. "Maybe we'll figure out what Dante was doing down there. And why he was so odd."

"I would not hold your breath." Arach frowned. "That is the correct phrase, is it not?"

I nodded. She was ancient enough and spent enough time sleeping beneath the castle that modern phases were difficult for her.

She smiled. "Excellent. Well, do not hold on to your breath. That was so long ago that I imagine the information is lost."

"That's fine," I said. "As long as we get that damned stone, I'm satisfied."

We finished the meeting quickly, with Jude updating us on the progress of everyone else. My sisters were busy collecting enough Seawort to protect all the cursed members for a short while, though they were having a hard time finding enough. The FireSouls had almost found the Fates, and I hoped they'd succeed. I'd rather bring the battle to them than the other way around.

After the meeting, Lachlan and I changed clothes in my apartment and then set out with the cats. Muffin's knowledge of the shortcuts through hell would give us a good jump on the Fates, if they, too, were after the stone already.

As the five of us walked down the sweeping staircase, I looked at Muffin. "Why were you in Dante's Inferno?"

How do you think I met my crew? He looked pointedly at Bojangles and Princess Snowflake III. *It was our first job, robbing level four.*

"What could you possibly want in hell?"

Oh, you'll see. Level four. He sounded wistful.

I wanted to ask for more detail, but we were already stepping out into the courtyard. Immediately, my gaze was drawn to the stone circle. It tugged hard at me, as if I needed to visit it. *Immediately.*

"Can you guys give me five minutes?" I asked. "I need to check something."

Lachlan looked at me quizzically but nodded. I needed no more encouragement. We couldn't spare much time—not with the Fates possibly there already, hunting for the stone—but I needed to check something.

I sprinted for the stone circle, the cool winter wind pulling at my hair. I pulled the gray jacket tighter around me, and it warmed me much more than a normal jacket.

The stone circle tugged harder at me the closer I got, the magic pulling me toward it. I stepped through the tall stones without hesitation.

Magic flared in the center of the circle, bright and fierce.

When it faded, I saw Sulis, the goddess of light who had been my de facto guide through this transformation.

Her serene gaze met mine. "You are changing."

"I am. Maybe." The words spilled out of me. I explained about the dream with the crow, and my lesson about changing fate.

Sulis nodded as if she weren't surprised. She opened her mouth to speak, but my mother appeared in the circle. Sulis glared at her.

"Mom!" I ran to her and hugged her. "Why are you here?"

She smiled, and her face was so wonderfully familiar that I grinned back. "I can feel when you enter the circle. I will always come."

"If you do not mind?" Sulis's voice was cutting. "I brought Ana here to tell her something important."

I pulled back from my mother, giving her arms one last squeeze, then looked at Sulis. "What do you know about my transformation?"

"You will inherit the powers of the Morrigan, but you must use them wisely."

"What's the Morrigan?"

"The Morrigan is a Celtic goddess of fate and war. She is the Battle Crow and is often represented as three, but you are one."

The Battle Crow. That made sense with my dream, and with my ability to change fate for the seal woman. And it also sounded really damned cool.

"Is that how I changed fate for the seal woman?"

"It is, though the Elders of the Indomidae helped you there. To change fate again, you must fully transform into a full Dragon God. When you do this, you will have the Morrigan's full powers. It will be the greatest and most important transition of your life."

Okay, no pressure. "How do I make that happen?"

"That is for you to find out. But you must embrace it. Do not fight it." Her gaze flicked to outside of the circle. "And do not dawdle. Time is of the essence."

"Thank you." I looked from her to my mother. After years without her, I would never be anything but happy to see her, even if she interrupted important meetings with gods. "I'll see you soon."

With that, I ran out of the circle, back to Lachlan and the cats.

"What was that about?" he asked.

I slowed, panting. "I'll get the powers of the Morrigan. Sulis just told me."

His brows rose. "Impressive. She's very strong."

"Good. I want to be strong. I *need* to be."

Especially where we're going. Muffin flicked his tail. *There is no time to waste. Tell your Boy Toy to take us to the peak of Mount Vesuvius on the western side.*

I glared at him but didn't tell him off for the Boy Toy comment since I didn't want to say the words in front of Lachlan. I turned to Lachlan instead. "Could you transport us to the western side of the peak of Mount Vesuvius? The entrance to Dante's hell is there, according to Muffin."

"I'm sure I'm not going to like this." He grinned.

I smiled back. He was probably right.

Lachlan's magic swelled as he created the portal, and the five of us stepped through. The ether sucked me in and spat me out on the other side of Europe.

Blisteringly cold wind whipped across my face as we stood amongst a cluster of volcanic rock.

Well done. Muffin paced around, inspecting our surroundings. *We're right near the portal, far from where the tourists visit.*

I looked at Lachlan. "He said you took us to the right place."

This way. Muffin stalked off between the cluster of rocks, and the four of us followed. Bojangles and Princess Snowflake III took the lead, a pep in their step. They were clearly excited to get back to hell.

Weird cats.

It didn't take long to find the right cluster of rocks. Dark magic spilled from the mouth of a gaping black hole that disappeared into infinity deep in the mountain. It was only about six feet wide, but it looked like it went on forever.

I shuddered at the horrible feeling on my skin. It felt like a thousand nails were being hammered into my body all at once, and tears pricked my eyes. "This is awful."

It's how you know you're in the right place. Muffin stood at the edge of the gaping black hole and looked down, his whiskers ruffling in the wind. *Now, we jump.*

I'd been afraid he'd say that.

The little cat didn't even hesitate. Just took a flying leap into the blackness. Bojangles and Princess Snowflake III followed, their delighted meows disappearing into the darkness.

I looked at Lachlan. "See you on the other side."

I jumped into hell.

9

The portal spat us out into the middle of a violent dust storm. Princess Snowflake III bowed her head as if she were used to the misery. Bojangles huddled up close to the fluffy white cat and stuck his face into her fur.

Come on! Muffin shouted. *We need to find my friends. They'll take us to the shortcut to the next level.*

I squinted my eyes against the blowing sand and followed Muffin. His little wings carried him above the ground as he led us towards a shadow in the distance. Lachlan wrapped an arm around me, and I huddled against his side. My jacket kept the worst of the stinging sand off of my skin, but anywhere that it hit my face or hands was awful.

We are almost there! Muffin bowed his head and flew onward.

The sand got into every crevice of my clothes, and my boots sank into it up to the ankles.

After trudging onward for a few minutes, I realized that we were approaching an enormous tent. It looked as if it were made of the hides of huge animals and sewn together with rough rope. A dim yellow light illuminated this world.

"Who lives in there?" I shouted, getting a mouthful of sand.

Muffin turned back, his green eyes glinting in the dim light. *The only people who will help us in this hellscape.*

"Thank fates for Muffin," I said. "We'd be screwed without a guide."

Princess Snowflake III hissed so loudly that I could hear it over the howling wind.

I looked down at her. "And you, too! And Bojangles."

Wouldn't want to hurt any of the cats' feelings. Not only did I like them, we needed them. I had no idea where to go in this realm.

We approached the tent, and the hides at the base whipped in the wind. Muffin found an opening in the side of the tent and slipped through, his little wings dragging against the leather. We followed him, stepping into a dimly lit interior that was full of people bustling about.

I squinted, letting my eyes adjust to the darkness. The ceiling was studded with glowing blue stones that shed an eerie light on the scene within. It looked just like a tiny village, shielded against the elements from outside.

Muffin flew through the crowd, heading unerringly toward the other side. Princess Snowflake III and Bojangles followed, skirting around the feet and legs of people who went about their business, chatting and bartering and heading wherever they were heading. Almost everyone was dressed in the same type of leather that made up the exterior of the tent. Some of them looked at us but said nothing. I couldn't tell if it was wariness or disinterest that kept them silent, but I didn't ask. Muffin was the boss here, and it was our job to follow along.

He led us to the far edge of the tent, where a figure was sitting on a rickety old chair, observing the hustle and bustle in the interior of the tent.

The man looked up as Muffin neared, his brown eyes widening. "Cat Sìth! You have wings now!"

An upgrade. Muffin fluttered up to the man and butted his head against his arm. It was the friendliest greeting that Muffin could make, so he must know this man well. *How are you, Aurius?*

"As well as can be, Cat Sìth. Why are you here?"

We need a ride to the shortcut that leads to level four.

The man grinned widely, revealing a mouth that was missing at least half his teeth. "You're in luck! We have a caravan going out in ten minutes." The man turned to look at Lachlan and me. "Who are your friends?"

Members of the Protectorate, and people on a mission. We need to get to the bottom of Hell as fast as possible.

The man grimaced. "I don't envy you that." He gestured for us to sit. "Join us. Can I offer you any refreshment? We have the finest swamp water and the tastiest dirt biscuits."

I grimaced and wondered if I should laugh at the joke. But it didn't actually seem like a joke. This was Hell after all. I took a seat on one of the low stools, Lachlan joining me.

"Thank you, but no," Lachlan said. "We have recently eaten."

The man leaned forward, the corners of his eyes crinkling. "First time in hell?"

"First time in this hell." I grinned. "It's not the worst one I've ever seen."

"That it is not. We are not so bad here. This is only level two. Most of us were jerks in life, so we ended up here. It's miserable, but it's not the worst. We've managed to make a pretty decent life."

"The same cannot be said of the lower levels?" Lachlan asked.

"Indeed not." The man laughed, a rusty sound.

"Have you seen two women come through? They would probably be dressed as Roman warriors. They are the Fates."

He frowned. "Haven't heard of their kind in these parts. Not in hundreds of years, at least. And if they'd been in level two recently, I'd know it."

So, hopefully we'd already beaten them to hell.

He looked at his wrist, as if there should be a watch there. There wasn't, but that didn't seem to matter to him. His gaze rose to meet ours. "You should go. The caravan will leave soon."

Muffin butted his head against the man's arm again, and then turned around to meet us. His little wings fluttered frantically as he tried to stay aloft. *Let's get a move on.*

We said goodbye to the man and followed Muffin across the tent. Princess Snowflake III and Bojangles followed us, staying close.

Muffin led us to an area at the far edge of the tent that looked like a stable. Horses that had been born with no eyes stomped impatiently at the dirt.

Muffin looked at me. *Rare Hell horses. They see in their own way and use their other senses to travel. Otherwise, the sand would be too much for them.*

"Cool." I turned my attention to the wagon that was hitched to the back of one of the Hell horses. There was a single bench at the front, and behind it, an arch-covered enclosure would protect the people or goods that were traveling across the sands.

"I feel like we're in the Wild West," Lachlan said.

"Yeah, that didn't work so well for the folks who tried to cross Death Valley in these things."

"Hopefully it will go better for us."

"It has to."

Muffin flew over to a woman who stood near the horse. She was almost entirely covered in leather garments. No sand was going to get to her skin. She had to be the driver.

Princess Snowflake III and Bojangles hopped up into the back of the wagon, disappearing behind the flaps of leather that acted as a door.

A moment later, Muffin turned to us, flying over. *Florencia says that she'll take us across.*

I looked at Florencia. She peered at me through a slit in her leather head covering, her blue eyes glinting sharply. "It'll be a deadly crossing."

"I'm used to that. Is there anything we can do to help?"

"Can you fight?"

"Yeah, pretty well." I hiked a thumb at Lachlan. "He's not so bad either."

The woman grinned. I couldn't see her mouth, but from the way her eyes crinkled, it was obvious. "Good, I like people who can fight. We need them down here."

I didn't know how she'd been enough of a jerk in her previous life to end up here, but she seemed pretty cool. Either way, I was grateful she was helping us.

She pointed to the back of the wagon, to the slit in the leather into which Princess Snowflake III and Bojangles had already entered. "You can get in there, and ride with Frank and Bill. Do whatever they say."

I nodded and climbed up into the wagon. The interior was larger than I'd expected, but it was filled with lumpy sacks of an unidentifiable substance. Two men sat on a tiny bench at the front of the wagon, each wearing the same leather outfit that Florencia wore.

The one on the right looked up at me. "Coming along for the ride?"

I found a seat on a tiny bench at the side. "Yes, looking forward to it."

He laughed at my joke and smacked his knee, then looked at his friend. "It's not often we get a funny one down here."

"You have low standards, Frank," grumbled the other one. He had to be Bill, if the laughing one was Frank.

I grinned. He was right—it hadn't been very funny.

Next to me, Muffin shifted uncomfortably, his little wings fluttering. On the floor, Bojangles was curled up, dead asleep amongst the bags of trade goods. Princess Snowflake III just looked bored.

There was a shout from outside, and the wagon began to rumble. It rolled forward, swaying lightly on its axles. As soon as we exited the large tent, I could feel it. Sand began to batter the wagon outside, and I shivered.

I looked at the two men. "This is a trading expedition?"

Frank nodded. "Yes, there's another settlement across the howling field of storms."

"We have to go through the dust storms," Bill said. "Then we go through the rainstorm. Then the snowstorm. Where are you headed?"

I looked at Muffin. "Ask him. He's the boss."

Muffin looked at the man. *We are headed to the shortcut to level four.*

Bill nodded, a grimace on his face. "Miserable place from what I hear."

There was something about this place that allowed other people to understand Muffin. I looked at Lachlan, but there was a confused crease at his brow. It seemed that even though we were here in the hellscape, only people from this realm could understand Muffin. I translated Muffin's words for Lachlan.

"Who built the shortcuts between the levels?" Lachlan asked.

"The desperate." Bill shook his head. "Though why you would want to go any lower in this damnable place, I have no idea."

We rumbled along for several minutes, the only sound the battering of the sand against the leather wagon cover. This was regular dustbowl shit, and that had been hell. Appropriate, really.

The cart rocked along as the wind whipped grains of sand

that began to work their way into our protected area. I looked at Lachlan. This might be miserable, but I liked adventures with him.

Soon, shouting sounded from outside. "Faster! Go faster, damn you!"

I looked at Frank and Bill, whose faces were lined with concern.

"There are a lot of dangers out there." Bill frowned, turning around to peek out of the wagon front. He was sitting directly behind the driver.

"Can't see anything," he muttered.

I'm going to go check it out. Muffin fluttered into the middle of the wagon and approached Frank and Bill. They parted to allow him to slip through the opening in the leather wagon cover and join the driver.

A few seconds later, he darted back inside, his green eyes wide. *Souls!*

"All hell." Fear flashed across Frank's face.

"What do you mean, souls?" I asked.

They're coming from up ahead. They're going to attack the wagon.

"Souls? Like phantoms?" Lachlan asked.

Not like phantoms. They hurt your body, not your mind.

Bill's face turned entirely white. "If they get a hold of us for too long, we'll become one of them. Our bodies will disappear, and we'll become nothing but formless ghosts, floating in misery with the winds on the plain."

I couldn't just sit there. We were being attacked. I had to help.

Lachlan clearly felt the same, because he was already moving toward the front, climbing over the bags of trade goods, nimbly avoiding stepping on a sleeping Bojangles.

Bill and Frank both shifted aside so Lachlan could pass through the slit in the leather out onto the driving bench.

"Your funeral," Bill muttered.

"Idiot." Frank shook his head.

I stood and scrambled across the bags.

"You too?" Bill asked.

I grinned. "Me too. Glutton for punishment, I guess."

Bill shook his head. "Both of ya, morons."

"It's not the worst I've been called." I climbed out through the slit in the leather, immediately wishing I had my sand goggles from back in Death Valley. The wind was howling out here, the sand flying so fast it stung like glass against my skin. I squinted my eyes nearly closed, hoping my lashes could protect me.

Florencia sat in the middle of the bench, hunched against the howling wind. Lachlan sat on her left side, so I took the right. From behind, Muffin peeked his head out of the slit in the leather, hiding behind Florencia's back.

"We're in trouble!" Florencia shouted. "Souls coming from up ahead."

I squinted into the distance, catching sight of a pale white glow.

"How do we fight them?" Lachlan shouted.

"You don't." Fear echoed in her voice. "No way to fight the incorporeal."

Never really seen them before. Muffin hissed. *Thought they were an old wives' tale.*

The wagon trundled along, the horse galloping as fast as it could.

"The horse will try to dodge them," Florencia said. "I'll do my best to steer around. And we hope."

Just hoping?

That sounded like a terrible plan.

I clung to the seat as we bounced along, every inch of exposed skin aching. The souls glowed brighter as they neared, until finally I could pick out individuals. They looked a bit like ghosts, but faceless and even more horrible.

Worse, they brought with them a darkness that made me shudder. It crept into my own soul, making despair fill me. I gasped, trying to focus on something good. Anything good. But I couldn't.

There was nothing but sadness and misery, spreading through my body like a plague.

"Does it always feel like this?" I shouted.

"Don't know!" Florencia spurred the horse on, shouting encouragement in Italian. "No one has ever survived the souls. Just rumors."

No one has ever survived.

We were only on level two. We couldn't die now.

Not only did we need to survive to save our friends, it would be damned embarrassing to go out this early in the game.

I watched the souls approach, glowing brighter with every yard they came nearer. The horse began to whinny, a sound of terror.

The souls were twenty feet away when the horse shrieked and veered right, trying to avoid them.

But they were fast, darting toward us.

Florencia pulled on the reins, trying to make the horse cut even farther to the right. But he was too slow. "We won't make it!"

The souls were only fifteen feet away now, so close that I could see the pale shimmer of their forms as they whirled on the wind. Sand howled around us, burning my outside as the souls burned my inside.

My heart thundered as the darkness closed in on my mind.

The souls brought with them a dark magic that felt impossible to escape.

But now that they were so close, I could feel their magic even more clearly. It was the opposite of everything I held dear. It was the opposite of *me*.

And it gave me an idea.

I called upon my power, reaching for the light that was deep within me. This was my core power, the gift from Sulis that gave me the light of life.

I fought against the darkness that spread from the souls, focusing on the light within me.

"Brace yourself!" Florencia shouted.

Muffin hissed.

I ignored them both, zeroing in on the light that was glowing outward from my chest. I let it fill my whole body, then forced it outward, toward the souls.

It blasted from me like an atomic bomb, lighting up the dim yellow world in a flash of light.

Florencia screamed.

I focused on pushing the light toward the souls. It was so bright that I couldn't see them, but I could feel their dark magic fading away.

I pulled back on my own magic immediately, not wanting to waste it. We had a long way yet to go.

When the glowing light disappeared, I gasped, inspecting my surroundings. The souls had gone, and even the sand had stopped whirling.

Florencia looked at me, eyes wide. "What the hell are you?"

"Dragon God."

"What's that?"

I was about to answer when the wind picked up, howling again, carrying even more sand than before. I shut my mouth, but not before I had a mouthful of sand.

Florencia leaned into the wind, driving the horse onward. I glanced back at Muffin.

He grinned at me, fangs glinting in the light. *Nice work. I've heard that no one has ever driven off the souls before.*

I shielded my mouth with my hand. "Let's hope they stay off. I blasted a ton of magic at them."

He nodded, then ducked back into the covered wagon.

"How far are we from the shortcut?" Lachlan shouted.

"About halfway there!" Florencia kept her head ducked against the sand, which seemed to be increasing.

It came faster and faster, so much of it that the world nearly turned dark.

"Something is wrong!" Florencia shouted. "Too much sand!"

"I've got this!" Lachlan shouted.

Thunder boomed overhead.

Florencia shrieked.

"Don't worry. *I* made the lightning!" Lachlan shouted. Rain began to fall, forcing some of the sand down, out of the air.

Florencia began to laugh. "It never rains here!"

Today wasn't a normal day.

Mud formed beneath the wheels of the wagon, but it kept rolling along, sending up sprays of the stuff. There was still sand whipping through the air, but the rain kept it minimal.

"Yah!" Florencia cracked the reins, and the horse ran faster, cutting through the mud.

With less sand in the air, the journey was easier. We rocked along, the wagon careening around boulders that appeared out of nowhere.

"We're nearly there!" Florencia shouted. "The terrain is changing."

The wagon veered right, and the energy in the air changed. There was something active in this area, a vibrating magic that made my hair stand on end.

I looked back toward the wagon to find that Muffin had once again peeked his head through the slit in the leather and was staring into the distance. *Feels like we're close.*

"Florencia said we are." I peered hard into the distance but couldn't see anything.

A few moments later, Florencia pulled the wagon to a stop. "This is as close as I can get you."

Muffin climbed onto the main bench and flew into the air, hovering in front of us. *I can lead the way from here.*

Lachlan and I climbed down off the buggy, and Princess Snowflake III and Bojangles followed.

"Have a good nap?" I asked the little orange cat.

He meowed, blinking sleepily.

I turned back to Florencia. "Thank you."

She nodded. "Best of luck to you. You're going to need it."

Frank and Bill poked their heads out of the wagon.

"Morons," muttered Frank.

"Idiots," said Bill.

I waved at them. "Bye!"

They scowled.

I turned to Muffin, who was already fluttering away.

He looked back, green eyes gleaming. *Come on! Hell waits for no one!*

10

Muffin led us through the desert, his head bowed against the wind. Once again, Bojangles pressed his face into Princess's thick fur as they trudged across the plain.

Muffin stopped at an area that looked no different than where we'd just been. If the magic hadn't been stronger here, I would have wondered why we were stopping at all.

"The shortcut is here?" Lachlan asked.

Right below me. Muffin fluttered above a patch of sand that looked the same as all the rest.

I pointed to it. "He says it's right below him."

Lachlan frowned. "Quicksand?"

"Could be."

Bojangles raced forward and leapt onto the sand. Immediately, he sank into it, the tip of his tail disappearing last.

"Looks like you're right." I grimaced.

Princess Snowflake had a sour expression on her face, no doubt due to the idea of getting a ton of sand in her fur. It was already a mess from the blowing grains, but I had a feeling the quicksand was going to be a real nightmare.

She stalked forward, her gait stoic, until she began to sink down into the golden sand.

Get a move on. Muffin pointed his tail toward the sand.

I followed Princess, gasping when my foot sank into the sand up to my calf. I glanced back at Lachlan. "See you on the other side."

This felt just like jumping into the Corryvreckan whirlpool. I hoped I survived this too.

The sand swallowed me up, rising past my knees, waist, shoulders, and finally my head. I took a deep breath and squeezed my eyes shut.

The world went black as I fell, and my stomach leapt into my chest.

When I landed on solid ground, I stumbled, going to my knees. I shook my head and brushed the sand off my eyelids, then opened them.

"Holy fates."

A world of gold spread out in front of me, endless fields of the shining yellow stuff. Mountains of it formed to my left and right, with a plain of gold in front. Even the sky had a yellowish tinge.

Lachlan fell to the ground next to me. He wiped the worst of the sand off his face as he stood. Muffin appeared at my side.

"This is where you ran a heist with Bojangles and Princess Snowflake, isn't it?" I asked Muffin.

Yep. The whole reason we came to hell.

"A dragon would love this place," I muttered to him.

No dragons here. Just misers and spendthrifts.

I turned to him. "What?"

"This is level four, where misers and spendthrifts spend eternity."

I frowned. "I would hardly say that merits a stay on the fourth level of hell."

This place is from the fourteenth century. They were weird back then.

"Aye, very." Lachlan inspected the area around us, his keen gaze alert for any dangers.

The gold glittered like the sun, and something tugged at my insides. I wasn't super into gold like a FireSoul was, but even I was interested in a place like this. It was like my Dragon God side was sitting up and taking notice of all the shiny shiny. My fingertips itched to take something, but I resisted.

There was no question that would go poorly. I'd read enough fairytales to know that.

A massive crash sounded in the distance, and I jumped. The sound was nearly deafening, and I raised my hands to my ears. "What's that?"

You'll see. Muffin began to fly ahead. *Come on.*

I hurried to join him, Lachlan at my side. "Anything I should know about this place?"

Plutus is the boss here.

"Who's he?"

Greek god of wealth. Not the worst bloke. We ran afoul of him when we tried our heist but made amends. Mostly.

Mostly? "I hope we won't run into a pissed-off god."

We might. But we're cool now. I think.

Great. "I think" was super comforting. I translated the information for Lachlan.

The ground was slick underfoot as we walked, the smooth gold gleaming bright. There was no sun up above that I could see, but somehow there was a yellow glow.

Bojangles raced ahead of us, sliding on the golden ground like he was in *Risky Business.* Princess Snowflake III stalked around, looking like she owned the place. That was a cat comfortable with luxury. Although luxury might not be the right word, since *everything* was made of gold. That'd make for some uncomfortable sitting and sleeping.

We skirted around some enormous piles of the glittery stuff, walking toward the sound of massive crashing objects. What was going on up ahead?

Finally, we made it around another huge pile of gold and caught sight of the action.

Two huge golden boulders were rolling toward each other, each pushed by a horde of people. As the boulders got closer and closer together, they picked up speed, until they finally smashed into each other so hard that they shattered, sending huge chunks of gold up into the sky.

They rained down upon us, and I dived left, barely avoiding one of the golden chunks that had to be the size of my torso.

It smashed into the ground next to me, making my bones vibrate.

"Bloody hell, that's dangerous." Lachlan climbed to his feet.

You've got to be fast.

"Muffin says you've got to be fast."

"Aye, he's right."

We have to get to the other side. Don't get hit.

It was easier said than done. Every few seconds, massive golden boulders were pushed toward each other. They came at uneven intervals, too, so it was hard to judge.

I told Lachlan what we had to do, and he nodded, a grim expression on his face. "Ready to get started?"

"Yeah." I glanced down at Bojangles and Princes Snowflake III, who were staring at the boulders, ready to run. "Let's go."

We sprinted across the smooth golden ground. I felt like Frogger or Mario in one of those old video games as I neared the crashing boulders. They smashed into each other so hard that the air itself seemed to vibrate, and chunks of them flew through the air.

I tried to keep my eye on them, but it wasn't easy with so many getting thrown around. My heart thundered in my ears as I dived and dodged.

"From the upper left!" Lachlan shouted.

I barely caught sight of the flash of gold in time, diving right to avoid the missile.

Bojangles dodged easily, and Princess Snowflake III used her new fire breath to melt anything that got in her way. At one point, I thought she was just having fun with it, racing toward the smaller boulders that rolled toward her and melting them with her flame.

From above! Muffin's shriek drew my attention to a huge golden rock that plummeted toward me.

I picked up speed, darting away from it.

More ahead!

He was right. More and more boulders were beginning to roll ahead of us, some seemingly of their own volition.

"We need to be faster!" A surge of magic accompanied Lachlan's words, and he shifted into his black lion form.

I darted toward him, and he crouched low. I jumped onto his back, and he sprang into action, racing ahead on strong legs. His gait was smooth and fast as he sprinted over the golden ground.

He dodged every boulder that rolled near us. Bojangles leapt over some of them, a big grin on his face, while Princess Snowflake III ran in front of us, clearing some of the way with her fire. When two huge boulders nearly blocked our way, she blasted her fire breath at them, and they melted into a puddle.

She leapt over the melted metal, white fur flying, and Lachlan followed. I clung tightly to his back, desperate not to fall over and land in the melted metal. That'd be a terrible way to go.

Almost there! Muffin flew overhead, darting and diving away from the flying chunks of metal. *Watch out on the left.*

Lachlan dived right, avoiding the speeding golden boulder.

From above!

I looked up, spotting a huge gold rock flying at us. Instinct drove me, making me reach deep inside for my control over the elements. I sent a blast of wind at the boulder, thinking how crazy the attempt was but trying it anyway. Wind couldn't be so strong that it would divert a boulder. But it shot out of me, so strong that it blew the boulder away.

"Holy fates." Awe surged through me as the boulder fell about twenty feet away. Good thing I'd followed that instinct.

I was getting stronger. My magic might still be only halfway there, but that was a definite improvement in my skills. Was it the Morrigan thing?

Lachlan leapt over a huge metal rock, then thundered forward on massive paws. I gripped his mane and crouched low over his back, the wind tearing at my hair.

Finally, we reached the end of the nightmarish video game scenario. Lachlan slowed to a halt, and I tumbled off of him onto shaky knees. I leaned against him, panting.

Muffin landed next to me. *Let the man shift, lady.*

I blinked. He was right. I stopped using Lachlan as my support structure, and he shifted back into human form.

He scraped a hand through his hair, a weary expression on his face. "Are we through?"

For now. Muffin's eyes narrowed on something in the distance.

"What is it?"

I don't know.

A figure walked toward us, gleaming and golden. He looked like he wore a toga of some sort.

I think it's Plutus. Crap.

"What got him stuck with this shitty job?"

Muffin winced. *Don't let him hear you say that.*

As Plutus neared, it became obvious that he was wearing a massive amount of golden jewelry. At first, I thought it might be that *he* was made of gold, but it seemed like he just had no self-control at the jewelry shop. He definitely didn't follow that old rule—take one accessory off before you leave the house.

Neither did I, in fairness, but my accessories were always weapons and my job was damned deadly, so I felt justified.

His stride was graceful and smooth, and when he stopped in front of us, he seemed to pause like a statue, displaying his limbs and his jewelry to their most graceful and obvious display.

Muffin shifted to stand behind me.

Perfect. That was definitely a good sign.

"That was quite the show." Plutus's voice was as smooth as melted gold.

"Thank you?" When I heard the question mark at the end of my words, I almost winced. But what did one say to that?

"Why are you here?" Plutus's gaze turned to Muffin. "And with the little thief, no less."

Muffin sauntered out from behind my legs. *Good to see you, Plutus.*

His brows—which had been painted gold—rose toward his golden hairline. "We're just going to ignore it, then?"

Works for me.

This conversation wasn't going well, so I jumped in. "We're seeking something to help our friends."

"They must be some friends, if you're willing to risk the levels of Dante's Inferno to reach them," Plutus said.

"They are." Lachlan looked at me like he'd do anything to save me. It warmed my insides like a big mug of hot cocoa.

It was interesting that Plutus called it Dante's Inferno. He'd explored the place, but he must have become quite famous here if they started calling it after him.

I was about to ask when Plutus spoke. "How far down are you going?"

"All the way." I pointed to Muffin. "We have a guide."

Plutus nodded. "And a good one at that, despite his sticky paws. You just might make it all the way. But I have something that might help you."

I frowned. "Why would you help us?"

Maybe the question was a bit rude, but I wasn't used to help from strangers.

"It's rare that I get such fine entertainment down here." He played with the heavy golden necklace at his throat. "Though my gold is usually entertainment enough. And I would also like you to get those cats out of here. I quite like where my gold is currently stored. *With me.*"

Muffin gave a toothy grin. *I won't touch a single ounce.*

"Thank you for any assistance," Lachlan said.

Muffin looked at me. *See, that guy knows how to be polite.*

A smile emerged on Plutus's face. He held out his arm, palm up. A golden sword appeared in his hand, and he held it out to Lachlan.

I couldn't help the grin that tugged up at the corner of my mouth. Lachlan was polite, so he got the golden sword. I liked that, to be honest. It gave a sense of order and rightness to this crazy place.

"This will help you on level five," Plutus said. "It is the only thing that will work against the fighters in the River Styx."

"What does that mean, exactly?" I asked.

Plutus smiled, but it was grim. "Oh, you will see."

"Oh, by the way. Have two Fates come through here? Roman ones."

He shook his head. "Not that I have seen or heard, and I see all in my level."

He sounded just like Aurius, Muffin's friend from level two. Hell wasn't short of confident men.

He pointed to a cluster of golden boulders about twenty yards away. "Now, begone with you. There's a long way left for you to travel, and I am a very busy man."

Busy with what, I had no idea, but I should be keeping my mouth shut in this realm. Of that, I was certain.

Thank you, your godliness. Muffin bowed his head.

Plutus waved his hand in a gesture that clearly said *yes, do go on about my awesomeness.*

I got the clue. I could be a bit thick sometimes, but I wasn't totally stupid. "Yes, thank you so much, Your Royal Eminence."

Plutus frowned. "Not royalty."

"Godly Eminence," I corrected.

He smiled. "Better."

"Thank you for the sword," Lachlan said.

Plutus waved it off. We departed, leaving him to gaze at the boulders that continued to crash behind us.

Muffin flew by my head. *That sword will be very helpful.*

"Good," I said. "I think we're going to need all the help we can get."

Bojangles trotted confidently up to a crack in the boulders, then slipped through the narrow space. Princess Snowflake III followed, and Muffin brought up the rear. Lachlan and I squeezed in behind them, entering a tiny open space between the boulders. I was no longer impressed by the splendor of so much wealth. It didn't mean anything down here. There was no way to spend it, so it was just a deadly yellow rock.

There was a hole in the middle of the space that was about four feet wide. The sides were made of smooth gold.

I crouched down and peered into it, taking in the smooth sides that sloped away. "It's a slide."

A fun one, too. Straight to level seven.

I looked at the sword that Lachlan had been given. "Are we skipping level five?"

The shortcuts are strange. Level four goes to level seven which goes to level five. Then to the bottom of hell.

"Thank fates we've got you as our guide," I said.

He preened, then turned back to the golden slide.

With a delighted meow, Bojangles leapt into the hole and was whisked away. Princess followed, stepping regally off onto the slide and then zipping away.

No dawdling. Muffin flew into my back as hard as he could, and I lost my balance and tumbled down the slide. He cackled as I slid downward so fast my eyes watered.

Wind tore at my hair as I slid down and down, farther and farther. I picked up speed with every meter, praying that it would be a soft landing.

The slide spit me out into a forest. I skidded across the ground, disturbing the leaves and twigs until I finally slowed to a halt.

Dizzy, I sat up next to Princess Snowflake III and Bojangles, both of whom looked like they'd had their brains rattled a bit. I probably looked the same.

Lachlan slid out next, somehow managing to rise gracefully to his feet. Muffin came last, laughing a weird, hissing cat laugh.

Slowly, I stood, taking in our surroundings. Above, lightning struck, thunder vibrating in the sky. It lit up the forest around us, which consisted of gnarled trees with no leaves. They were creepy fairytale-looking trees, and the ground was scattered with thousands of dead leaves.

"Well, aren't you an arse-faced old bag." A crotchety voice sounded from behind me, and I spun, searching for the person.

I saw no one. Just a bunch of old trees. "Who the hell said that?"

"The hippo's ball sack wants to know who spoke!"

Hippo's ball sack? I grimaced. Gross.

I squinted into the darkness, finally catching sight of the gleam of eyes.

"It's a tree," Lachlan murmured.

He was right. There was a face right in the tree, about midway up the trunk, and it was glaring at me.

Slowly, I approached the tree. "What climbed up your roots?"

The face made of bark twisted, and a surprised laugh burst out of it, sounding rusty and rarely used. "Climbed up my roots?" The tree slapped the ground with a limb, as if he were slapping his knee. "Never heard that one before."

"I don't imagine you get out much," I said.

The tree laughed again.

Muffin shot me an appraising look. *You're on a roll. He likes you.*

"I wouldn't go that far, cat." The tree glared at him, then turned his gaze back to me. He whipped out a limb toward me, smacking me in the shoulder.

Pain flared, and I slapped my hand to the injury. "Ouch!"

The tree's bark-brows rose. "That's a nice jacket. My limb should have cut right through it."

I frowned at him. "You were going to cut me? I didn't do anything to you. And now you're complimenting my jacket?"

What a weirdo.

I knew better than to speak *those* words out loud, though.

"Someone powerful must favor you if you have that jacket." The tree moved a branch to the hem of my jacket and rubbed the material.

I stepped back. "No touching. And yes, someone powerful did favor me with this jacket."

The tree's gaze moved to Lachlan, glued to the golden blade

that hung from his hand. "And that sword! Plutus gave that to you."

"Aye, he did."

A crafty gleam entered the tree's eyes. "I like the powerful."

A screech sounded in the trees, loud and sharp. I winced at the sound, pain shooting through my eardrums. The tree winced, too, an annoyed look of wariness entering his eyes as he raised his gaze to the sky.

"Death flies above." Dread echoed in his voice.

11

I followed his gaze, catching sight of a figure hovering high in the air. Massive wings were silhouetted by the moon, attached to the figure of a person. Well, maybe a person. I squinted up into the sky.

What the hell was that? A demon?

"Curses, it's a harpy." The tree scowled up at the sky.

The harpy dived, her powerful wings carrying her down toward the tree. Up close, I could spot her beak, and the evil glint in her beady black eyes. She raised a blade of black metal and struck out at the tree's branches.

The tree deflected her blade with a limb, but a grimace flashed across his face. He struck out with another branch, driving her back up into the sky.

I frowned. "Why is she attacking you? You did nothing to her."

"It keeps her entertained." The tree scowled up at the harpy and waved his branches in a threatening manner. "Be gone, fowl wench!"

Okay, maybe that's why she was attacking. I didn't want to be called a foul wench either. Or did he mean *fowl*, like birds? She did have wings. And she *had* started it. She should just hurl insults back, not lead with the sword.

"That's hardly fair, considering you're stuck here on the ground," Lachlan said.

"I hold my own." The tree turned a considering gaze toward us. "Hmmm. If you will get rid of that harpy for me, I will help you with the next level of hell."

That was an interesting offer. I could probably handle a harpy, but I didn't know what was coming next in hell. Probably something terrible.

I looked at Muffin, who nodded. Though honestly, I didn't really need the bribe. The tree might be a miserable bastard, but it wasn't fair for the harpy to attack like this.

And just for entertainment? Nope, I didn't like that. "Okay, we'll help you."

"Aye, don't like the unfairness of it." Lachlan scowled at the harpy above.

My gaze followed his, drawn to the sight of gleaming black wings. Something tugged in my chest, a sense of knowing. A sense of familiarity.

Mine.

"I'll drive her away with a storm," Lachlan said.

I could fly up and scratch her. Muffin raised a paw, nails glinting.

Both were good ideas, and I tried to focus on them. But my mind was drawn to the harpy, and I couldn't stop staring at her wings. My back began to ache, as if something should grow from it.

I blinked. That was weird.

Lachlan raised his hands, his magic surging on the air. The scent of the forest swelled, making this dead place suddenly feel more alive.

Normally, I would suck the scent into my lungs, but right

now, I could only focus on the strange feeling inside my chest. On my obsession with the harpy's wings.

Frankly, I had the strongest desire to shift, and transform into something else.

That was freaking weird.

I wasn't a shifter.

The dream I'd had flashed in my mind.

I am a crow.

Magic exploded within me, an earthquake that shook my very being. I nearly fell to my knees as it surged through me. Rain began to fall in the clearing, Lachlan's magic beginning to create a storm.

But I couldn't focus on that. All I could focus on was the vision of a crow in my mind. Black feathers, strong claws, sharp beak.

Suddenly, I was flying.

I was above the ground.

Holy fates, I was in the freaking air.

Holy tuna! Muffin's exclamation barely penetrated my consciousness.

The world looked different from here. I had better vision. Clearer vision. I looked down to see Lachlan staring up at me, shock in his eyes.

I opened my mouth to speak, but the only thing that came out was a loud screech.

"Terrible and great." The tree's words echoed up toward me.

Terrible and great.

The words rang a bell, but I ignored them, looking away from my friends below and turning my gaze up to the sky, searching for the harpy. She flew above, silhouetted by the moon.

She shrieked, a battle cry of pure rage, and dived toward me.

I moved my wings, awkward at first, but gaining strength and coordination as I rose higher in the sky.

I flew through the trees, the branches scraping at my wings. I ignored them, the thrill of flying carrying me up toward the harpy.

Up close, I could see that she wore a breast plate made of scales and had long claws and fangs. Her sword was made of some kind of strange black metal, and she raised it as she neared me.

I flew toward her, opening my beak to screech a battle cry.

This felt so natural. Every second, I grew stronger and more coordinated. Fighting in the air was like breathing. *Flying* was like breathing.

Joy surged in my chest, a lightness of being that was at odds with battle.

Or was it?

I didn't care. All I cared about was the fight.

I will win.

The harpy swung her blade for me, but I deflected with my talons, forcing the sword away. I snapped my beak at the harpy's wings, but she was too fast, jerking them away.

The harpy darted back, wheeling on the wind, then returning to me, faster than ever. We clashed again, my talons digging into her thigh as her sword swiped across my chest.

The harpy shrieked, the noise so harsh and loud that my ears felt like they were bleeding. It hurt so badly that I almost didn't feel the pain in my chest as blood poured from my wound.

I darted away from her, using my wings to carry me a few yards away.

The harpy charged me again, and I flew to meet her, clashing in a tumble of claws and beaks. I swiped at her blade with my claws, knocking it away. The black metal fell through the air, disappearing below.

The harpy struck out with her own claws, slicing them across my wing.

Pain flared, but I ignored it, aiming a bite at her wing. This time, my beak made contact, and I crunched down on her wing. She shrieked again, and the sound nearly sent me falling from the sky. I released my bite on her wing.

I ignored the pain as best I could and kicked her with my feet. She tumbled away, falling through the air until her wings managed to get her upright. She glared at me, her black eyes full of evil, and hissed a curse that I didn't recognize. Then she turned and flew off into the night.

I took in my surroundings, my wings now keeping me effortlessly aloft. Flying was becoming more natural. The wind in my feathers felt like a homecoming.

Holy fates, I was really the Morrigan. The Battle Crow.

I was terrible and great. The tree had said so, and somehow, those words had registered deep within my soul.

I looked down at the trees below, catching sight of my companions staring up at me. Lachlan seemed impressed, and so did Princess Snowflake III. Bojangles looked bored, and Muffin's gaze was scanning the surroundings, no doubt scouting for danger.

I flew back down to them, nimbly avoiding the tree branches that had scratched me before. As I neared the grounds, I felt compelled to change back into my human form. The desire fueled me, more than just a rational need to become human and speak my thoughts again. It was like I *needed* to be human if I stood on the ground. As I neared the earth, the magic surged within me once again. By the time I reached the forest floor, I was human. The transition was seamless.

I reached up to check the wound at my chest, but it was gone. The harpy's blade had definitely cut me, but the wound had disappeared.

Did shifting make it disappear?

If so, that was a sweet perk.

Even better, I wasn't naked. It was good to know that I retained my clothes and possessions after shifting. It would be seriously inconvenient to end up naked after every battle.

Lachlan looked at me, questions in his eyes, but he kept his mouth shut about the change. So did I. We didn't need to show any weakness in front of the tree, and suddenly changing into an entirely new species for the first time was kind of a weakness.

I turned to the tree and crossed my arms. "Well, I took care of the harpy."

The tree gave me an appraising glance. "I can't say that I expected that. But you did do the job." He lowered a branch again, and I stiffened, expecting him to whip it out at me. I was not in the mood to get another hit. Instead, he used another branch to break off a piece and handed me the slender limb of the tree. It was no more than a quarter inch thick and six feet long. "That will help you at the River Styx."

I looked down the branch. "How will it help?"

"Oh, you will see."

I looked up, frowning. That was exactly what Plutus had said, and it was freaking annoying.

"Have two Fates come through here?" Lachlan asked.

"Roman Fates?" The tree frowned. "No. Not that I have seen. And I—"

"See all in your realm?" I finished for him.

He scowled. "Exactly." Then he closed his eyes, and the face disappeared. It just looked like a regular tree now.

That's it. He's done. Might as well get a move on. Muffin turned and flew away.

"Damn." I shrugged and met Lachlan's gaze. "At least we know we are probably ahead of the Fates. That's three levels we haven't seen them on."

He nodded, and we turned to follow Muffin. Princess Snowflake III and Bojangles kept pace with us as we walked through the creepy forest. I was certain that I heard whispers as we walked, and they no doubt came from the trees themselves, but none of them spoke directly to us.

The screech of harpies sounded in the sky high above, and occasionally I caught sight of something dark streaking past the moon. This whole place was eerie. A true nightmare forest.

Even Princess Snowflake III didn't seem to like it. The white fur on her back stood straight up as she trotted along. As usual, Bojangles didn't seem to notice. But that was just Bojangles.

My mind raced with the memory of turning into the Battle Crow.

Lachlan shifted to walk closer to me and spoke in a low voice. "Was that the first time you've turned into a giant crow?"

"Yeah. It's part of my transition to the Morrigan, but I have no idea how I made it happen."

"Well, it was impressive."

This is it. Muffin landed on the ground and stared at a pool of black oil.

I stopped at the edge of the pool, which was about ten feet across and gleamed with a dark light. "Oh, gross. Are we supposed to jump in that?"

You bet your tuna we're jumping in that.

Princess Snowflake III looked at the black pool in despair. Clearly she had been here before. I couldn't blame her. It would be a pain to clean myself off. But with her white fur? She was definitely going to be spending a long time in the bath.

Might as well jump in. Muffin followed his words with action and leapt into the black oily pool. He disappeared half a second later, his head sinking below the surface.

I sucked in a bracing breath and jumped in after him, not

wanting to wait. It was going to suck, so I might as well get it over with.

Just before the black oil sucked me down, I pinched my nose, shut my mouth, and closed my eyes. I gripped the branch tightly, not wanting to lose the tree's gift, even though I didn't know what it was capable of.

The oil closed around me, slick and cold. My heart thudded, claustrophobia gripping me, a feeling that I almost never had. But the oil was quick, sucking me down and whooshing me away. I spilled out into another realm, one that was lit with a blood-red sky.

I gasped, climbing to my feet. Every inch of me was coated in a layer of black oil. It smelled so bad that I nearly gagged. Muffin shook himself violently, sending sprays of black oil onto the ground around him. It didn't clean him entirely, but he was able to fly into the air and hover in front of my face.

This sucks.

"Yep."

Lachlan appeared next to me, followed by Bojangles and Princess Snowflake III. All of them looked miserable, slick with the black liquid.

I turned my attention to our surroundings.

The sound of the battle echoed in the air. Something in that sound called my soul, a strange tugging sensation. A feeling of familiarity. It reminded me of the dream where I had heard the battle while in crow form. In the dream, I'd understood that I had control over the battle.

What does that even mean?

"Let's go." Lachlan started forward, golden sword gripped in his hand.

I clutched my branch, having no idea what to do with it, and followed him. The cats kept pace, dripping oil as they walked.

Ahead of us, a battle was being fought in the middle of the

River Styx. Thousands of individuals swung swords and fists while standing knee high in the rushing water. Blood sprayed like it was rain.

The fight was vicious. But most horrible of all was the joy in the air.

We stopped about twenty feet from the river.

"They like it." Confusion sounded in Lachlan's voice. "I enjoy a good fight myself every now and again. But this is a true nightmare."

He was right. The sky was as red as blood and smelled strongly of sulfur. This battle looked like it had raged for centuries. For millennia. People died left and right, only to be resurrected again to continue fighting.

But their joy in the act was unmistakable, and so was their rage.

Muffin meowed. *We have to cross the river.*

"Looking forward to it." *Not.* There were so many fighters in the river that I had no idea how we would get through.

Could I shift back into the form of the Battle Crow? Lachlan could ride on my back as I went across. I had a ridiculous vision of carrying a basket in my beak that was filled with the Cats of Catastrophe.

I shook the crazy image away and tried to call on the same magic that had turned me into a crow before.

I felt nothing.

I reached deeper into myself, trying to pull on the magic, trying to drag it out from within myself. I imagined shifting into the Battle Crow and flying over the battle, then delivering my friends safely to the other side.

But nothing happened. The magic that had filled me so recently was gone.

"Are you trying to turn back into a crow?" Lachlan asked.

I looked at him. "Yeah. How'd you know?"

"It's the only logical thing. And you were weirdly silent for a while."

"It's not working. I just wish that I had enough control."

"It's a transition," Lachlan said. "It hasn't happened fully yet, but it will."

"How do I *make* it happen?"

Mystery of the ages, Muffin meowed.

Lachlan nodded. "What he said."

"I'll have to figure it out. But for now, let's use the tools that we have."

Lachlan held the blade out toward me. "Here, you take this."

I shook my head. "No, Plutus gave it to you. He did it for a reason."

"Just take it."

"No." I raised my branch. "I have a deadly and fearsome weapon."

Sure you do.

I looked at Muffin. "Enough from the peanut gallery. My stick will save the day."

I wasn't so sure of that, but I wasn't about to take the sword from Lachlan.

Onward! Muffin flapped his wings, looking weirdly excited.

Princess Snowflake III led the way toward the battle, trotting along with some serious pep in her step. She was going to enjoy this, I could already tell. It'd distract her from the black oil coating her fur, at least.

As we neared the battle, the sound of clanging swords echoed louder in the air. The shrieks of the dead and dying made me shiver, and the joy in the laughter of the fighters was one of the darkest things I'd ever heard.

"Stay close to me," Lachlan said.

"You don't have to tell me twice."

As a group, we approached the river. Bojangles hurtled ahead, racing toward the fight. He meowed in glee, then leapt onto the back of the nearest fighter. He disappeared, using his new invisibility magic, but it wasn't hard to see the path that he took through the fighters. The screams and spraying blood made it obvious enough.

He cleared the way for us, an invisible whirlwind of claws and teeth.

Lachlan stepped into the river, and Princess Snowflake III took a running leap and jumped onto his right shoulder. A blast of fire shot from her mouth, and she began to help Bojangles clear the path in front of us.

"Wow, that's super handy." It was like having our own feline blowtorch. The fighters in front of us fell away, opening a path for us to cross.

I stepped into the river, following closely behind Lachlan.

Fighters surged toward us from the sides, turning their attention to us.

Lachlan used the golden sword to fight them off, swinging so fast and so gracefully it looked like a dance.

It was the strangest sight, to see such a skilled fighter with a fire-breathing cat riding on his shoulder, both of them coated in slick black oil.

Sometimes, my life was ridiculous, but I wouldn't trade it for anything.

I gripped the tree branch in my hand, waiting for it to come alive or do something. When one of the fighters stumbled towards me, gleaming blade raised in his hand, I struck out with the tree limb, aiming for his chest.

It slapped against him and did nothing.

Crap! I dived left, narrowly avoiding his blade. Muffin, who had been flying by my head, swiped out for the man, raking his claws across his face and then kicking him with his strong hind legs.

The man fell backward into the water, a massive splash rising up.

"Okay, so the tree branch is not a fighting weapon." I scowled at it.

Nope! Muffin darted for another attacker, driving him off, while Lachlan kept up the fight ahead.

But more fighters surged towards us, nearly a dozen of them, enough that they were going to bowl us over. Panic sent my blood racing.

I tried to use my magic to call on the river, and bend it to my will, but it didn't work. Unlike other water, the river lay silent and dormant, unwilling to follow my commands.

No huge surprise there. Not only was it not normal water—it was the freaking River Styx for fates' sake—it was mostly made of blood.

When the fighters neared, I called upon my old shield magic, hoping to drive them back.

Nothing happened.

Surprise raced through me.

I tried again, but nothing came.

My heart leapt. If my shield magic was gone, did that mean I was fully transitioning to Dragon God?

I didn't have time to dwell. The attackers were too close. I drew a sword from the ether, swinging for the nearest fighter. It passed right through him without doing any harm.

Crap!

Plutus had been right. Only the golden sword would work against these fighters.

I staggered along behind Lachlan, dodging anyone who came too close. Muffin had my back, using his fangs and claws to drive off the attackers. He had no trouble fighting down here. But then, this was his domain.

We were only halfway across, and the onslaught of fighters was getting worse. Fear iced my muscles and chilled my skin.

I was worthless back here, unable to fight. I had to try something.

I called upon old faithful, the light within me that seem to drive off anything made of darkness. And these fighters... They were made of darkness. Only the truly evil would take such joy in killing. This was not normal bloodlust, or the crazed obsession of the Norse berserkers. Or even the delight of the Cats of Catastrophe. This was just evil.

The magic swelled within me, the light rising to the surface. I could feel that it was the last of my magic, the dregs of what was in my soul.

The light burst out of me, driving the fighters back. There were so many of them, and I was so weak. I must have used up most of my magic already. Fear thundered through me as I worked, sending my light toward the attackers.

I was only able to drive off a dozen, but Bojangles kept up his devilish work, while Princess Snowflake III continued to clear the path with her fire. Lachlan was as quick as ever with the golden sword.

I searched for the other shore. We were more than halfway across. *We are going to make it.* I called on even more magic, using everything I had to help us get across.

Then something grabbed my ankles and yanked me under. I lost my footing so fast that I didn't even have time to scream. Somehow, Lachlan saw me and grabbed my arm right before I went under.

Then his legs were knocked out from under him. The last thing I saw before I went under entirely was him getting yanked down as well. Princess Snowflake III clung to him as we all disappeared under the surface of the river.

12

The disgusting bloody water closed around my head, and panic flared in my chest.

Around my legs, hands clawed at me, pulling me deeper. There were people beneath the river.

There were bodies down there, continuing the fight underwater.

Fear like I had never known rose in my chest. I nearly opened my mouth to scream, and barely resisted sucking in the dirty water.

Instinct drove me to raise the branch that I clutched in my hand. I gripped it as tightly as I could and felt unfamiliar magic vibrate through my palm.

Then it tugged. I gripped the branch tighter and grabbed Lachlan with my other hand, making sure that we were connected.

The branch pulled at me, and I kept my grip tight. It began to pull us through the water, breaking the grasp of those who held us down. I burst out of the river, gasping raggedly and opening my eyes.

The branch had turned into a rope and was wrapped around

a rock on the far side of the river. It pulled us out of the water, dragging us toward the shore. Princess Snowflake III clung to Lachlan's back, her eyes wild and pissed. Bojangles and Muffin waited for us on the other side of the water.

When we reached the rocky shore, the rope turned back into a regular branch. I scrambled up onto the rocks, leaving the river far behind me. I gasped and collapsed on the ground, panting.

Lachlan landed beside me, catching his breath.

Holy tuna, that was close. Muffin looked at the stick with wide eyes. *That's some stick you have there.*

A second later, the stick disintegrated, turning into dust.

"Well, I guess that was one-time-use magic." I flicked the dust with my finger, and it blew away. Slowly, I sat up.

Lachlan did the same. "At least we're clean."

I laughed. "Sort of."

I wasn't sure what was worse, the black oil from the shortcut or the bloody water of the River Styx. I was going to need a dozen baths when I got home.

Princess Snowflake III shook herself so fiercely that water flew in every direction.

Together, we staggered to our feet. I was so exhausted that I could hardly move. I turned and observed the fight in the river. The combatants continued their deadly, endless battle. None of them spared a glance for us, which was fine by me. I was totally out of energy, and totally out of magic.

I looked at Lachlan. "How are you?"

"Completely out of magic. We need to rest, or we won't survive the rest of this realm."

"Do you think we can afford to lose the time?"

"I don't think anyone could have made it here before us, so we should be ahead of the Fates. They don't know the shortcuts like we do. We'll beat them to the stone."

I turned to Muffin, weakness pulling at me. "I'm tapped out. Is there anywhere that we can rest? Just for a little while. Just long enough to recoup our magic."

You're in luck. I've got just the place. Muffin launched himself into the air and began to fly away from the river. He was really getting better at the flying thing. Now, he could maintain a height of about six feet off the ground, only bobbing down occasionally.

He led us away from the battle, across the barren fields of dead grass. It still smelled of sulfur, but there was sadness to the air here as well.

In the distance, a low hill rose up from the ground. Muffin went straight to it, flying for a cluster of boulders against the side.

This is an excellent hidey-hole. He flew through a crack in the rock, disappearing into the darkness.

I didn't even hesitate. I followed him right in, ready to rest in any hidey-hole he might find. Lachlan and the cats followed me into the darkness. I shook my hand, igniting the magic in my lightstone ring. It gleamed on our surroundings, illuminating a narrow tunnel through the rock. Princess Snowflake III trotted ahead of us, followed by Bojangles. They knew exactly where we were going, and they wanted to get there quick.

I picked up my pace, following them deeper into the earth.

The tunnel opened into a large cavern. A beautiful blue pond glittered on the far side, reminding me of the pond that had been in Aerdeca and Mordaca's underground lair. Behind it, a soft bed of green moss spread over the ground. Vines crept up the wall on the left, ripe red fruit hanging from the branches.

You can eat the Night Apples, Muffin meowed. *Tastes fine, won't kill you.*

"My two primary requirements." I grinned. "You're *sure* we can eat the food in hell?"

Would I lie to you?

"Depends."

Well, not about this, so eat up.

I passed the message on to Lachlan as Muffin flew toward another small tunnel that exited the cavern on the far-right side. Bojangles and Princess Snowflake III followed him.

We're off to visit friends. You're safe here. See you in a few hours. With that, he disappeared, flying off through the exit, his hairless tail the last thing to disappear.

"They're off to visit friends for a few hours," I said.

Lachlan frowned. "Friends? Here?"

"Is it really that surprising that my hairless, winged, thief-cat has friends in hell?"

"No, actually, it's not."

I grinned and walked over to the apples, then pulled one from the vine and bit in. An explosion of flavor filled my mouth, and I swallowed quickly. "These are delicious."

Lachlan plucked one, and we chowed down, filling our bellies. As soon as I was finished, I took off my clothes. I felt so filthy from the River Styx that I didn't even consider modesty, just stripped down and raced for the pond.

I jumped in with a splash, gasping at the bubbly warmth that flowed around me.

"You look happy." Lachlan's gaze heated. "And damned good."

I grinned at him, then splashed water in his direction. "Why don't you join me?"

He smiled, so handsome that he took my breath away, and stripped out of his clothes. He made his way into the water, and my realization from before blared into my mind.

I loved him.

I'd hesitated to tell him before because I'd been scared. It hadn't been the right time, either, but fear had been my primary motivator for silence.

I couldn't be scared anymore. Not when there was so much at stake. The Protectorate, our friends, our lives. There was no time to waste.

He drifted toward me through the water, his gaze devouring me. His cheekbones were sharp in the dim light of the cave, his lips full. The heat in his eyes made me blush, but there was something else there. A softness that I hadn't seen before.

He reached out and drew me to him, his gaze meeting mine.

I opened my mouth to tell him that I loved him, but he spoke first.

"I love you, Ana." His voice was deep and sure.

Shock lanced me. "Really?"

"Of course. You're strong and brave and smart and beautiful. You're the best person I've ever met, and I love you. No question."

He'd beaten me to it. Warmth filled my chest, so much of it that I thought I would float away. I wrapped my arms around his neck. "I love you, too. I wanted to tell you before, but I chickened out."

He grinned. "I love you, even if you are a chicken."

I laughed and pressed my lips to his. He groaned and pulled me closer, his arms tightening around my waist. I pressed myself against his warmth, reveling in his strength.

The kiss stole my breath, and when he lifted me up and laid me on the soft bed of moss, I thought I'd died and gone to heaven. The last thing I'd expected was to confess my love in hell, but life was crazy with Lachlan. Dangerous, but crazy and perfect.

～

THE DREAM CAME AGAIN. It had that same kind of hazy reality that made it obvious I was no longer in the real world. I wore the long green dress. It flapped around my ankles as I strode across the open countryside.

My gaze was riveted to the cliff ahead of me where the seagulls whirled on the air, squawking and calling to the morning breeze.

I would join them.

I began to run as fast as I could across the rolling green grass. The wind tugged at my hair as I picked up speed. I neared the cliff with no sign of slowing down.

Holy fates, I was going to jump off of it.

I tried to stop myself, the conscious part of me not wanting to throw myself off the cliff. But dream-me was determined to do the deed.

Why?

Waves crashed far below, and I realized that they were so far down I would be dead as a doornail when I hit the bottom.

But I kept running anyway. Nothing could stop me. I reached the edge of the cliff and leapt into the air, then plummeted toward the sea. My heart jumped into my throat, and the wind made my eyes tear up. Panic closed around my throat, so tight that I couldn't even scream.

Half a moment later, I was swooping upward. My huge black wings caught the breeze, and I was gliding along with the seagulls, skirting over the waves.

Holy fates! I was the Battle Crow.

Believe.

Risk.

The words echoed in my mind, but I didn't understand them. Believe in what? Myself?

I did, didn't I?

With the wind in my feathers and the world spread out

below me, it was hard to focus on anything but the joy of flying. I was high in the air, letting the earth fall away. On a strong gust of wind, I turned back to the shore.

Only then did I realize that it was the Protectorate castle spread out far below me. I had been running across our lawn, headed straight for the cliffs that fell into the sea at the back of the castle grounds.

My gaze was drawn unerringly towards the stone circle. The huge gray rocks speared toward the sky, ancient and majestic. I would always be drawn to that place. Always. I flew toward it, swooping low over the stones and thinking of my mother and all the Druids that had come before me.

Would I be worthy of them?

Believe.

Risk.

akey, wakey! Muffin's yowl cut through the haze of my dream. His shriek tore me away from the joy of flying through the Scottish sky. I jerked upright, blinking sleep from my eyes.

We were still in the beautiful cave deep in the depths of hell. The blue light of the pond glittered, highlighting Bojangles, who somehow managed to float on his back in the still water, a blissful expression on his face. Princess Snowflake III watched him with disdain. Muffin sat next to me on the plush green moss, his green eyes glued to me.

We better get a move on. You've been sleeping long enough. He gave me a critical look.

I stretched. "You're right."

Next to me, Lachlan rose, grace in every movement. Briefly, my gaze caught with his, and worlds flowed between us. But now was not the time to discuss last night, especially not with an audience made up of the Cats of Catastrophe.

I could only imagine what Muffin would say, and I knew I didn't want to hear it.

"How far from the shortcut are we?" Lachlan asked.

Not far. It will take us straight to the bottom level of hell, where we should be able to find the Doomsday Stone.

I turned to Lachlan and translated Muffin's words.

He nodded and grinned, satisfaction on his face. "Good, I'm ready to get the hell out of this place."

"I couldn't agree more." I climbed down off the bed of moss and walked over to the vines that grew along the rock wall of the cave. I pulled down several of the bright red fruits and handed a couple over to Lachlan. We ate as we left the cave, the cats leading the way out of the tunnel.

We stepped outside, and hell was as bad as I remembered. The blood-red sky was as bright as ever, a threatening shade that evoked memories of battle and death.

This way. Muffin flew off, skirting around the edge of the rocks. Bojangles raced after him, followed by a more sedate Princess Snowflake III.

Lachlan and I followed, making quick progress over the uneven ground.

We weren't far from the cave entrance when my comms charm blared to life. Magic crackled in the air, and Bree's voice echoed from the charm. "The Fates are attacking! They've gathered outside the walls. What's your progress?"

Oh shit. Panic made my stomach drop. "We're almost to the Doomsday Stone. Just one more level to go."

"Hurry," she shouted. "The Fates have gathered their troops outside the castle walls. They haven't broken through yet, but it won't take them long. There are hundreds of them."

Why were they attacking now if they didn't have the Doomsday Stone? They needed that to make the curse on the tattooed ones permanent. Unless they'd already stolen the stone from hell? Had they beaten us to it?

My gaze met Lachlan's, and I swallowed hard. We never should've taken last night to rest.

We'd had no more magic and had been exhausted beyond belief, but we should have pressed on.

As if he knew what I was thinking, he said, "We couldn't have kept going. We never would've survived, and that would've been worse. We'll make it in time. Have faith."

"What's he saying?" Bree asked

"We'll make it in time, I promise."

"Just hurry. We'll hold them off as best we can."

"Good luck. I love you."

"Love you back. Be careful."

I cut the connection with the comms charm, and we began to race across the dark ground. I prayed the Fates hadn't gotten to the stone before us. Muffin flew as fast as he could, and we kept pace. My lungs burned as I sprinted over the rough ground, the sulfurous air making it hard to breathe.

Almost there! Muffin flew faster.

I pushed harder, managing to keep up. Bojangles was far ahead, racing across the rocky ground and leaping over boulders. Princess Snowflake III ran right behind him, a white blur against the dark landscape.

Muffin stopped in front of a cluster of black rocks. I joined him, looking down into a gaping black hole. The edges were made of jagged black stone, each looking sharp enough to cut.

We've got to go down there.

"Can't say I'm surprised." I began to climb immediately, scrambling down the rocks. I did my best to stay away from the sharp edges, but couldn't avoid them all. The rocks cut painfully into my palms as I climbed. Fortunately, my jacket protected my torso and arms from any damage.

Lachlan followed, moving quickly and gracefully down the side of the tunnel. The cats had no problem avoiding the sharp edges. But then, they were cats.

Farther and farther we climbed, and the air grew colder and

the smell of death stronger. Eventually, ice began to cover the rocks. At first, it was a relief. It was smooth and cool and felt good against my wounds. But soon, I started slipping. My foot lost its hold, and I slid down several rocks. Somehow, I managed to grab one and stop myself from falling farther.

Lachlan looked down at me, concern in his gaze. "Let me go first."

"So that I can fall on you and force you down?"

He'd make a great mattress if you fell all the way.

"No." I kept climbing, scrambling down the icy rocks as quickly as I could. But soon, they were too slick from a combination of my blood and ice. Even Lachlan lost his grip above me, managing to stop himself before he took me out on a dangerous slide down the tunnel.

"I'm going to try to melt some of the ice." Carefully, I fed some of my heat into the freezing stuff. It began to melt, cold water flowing down around my boots. The jagged rock surface was revealed, and I gripped it, wincing. But this was better. At least this way, I wouldn't go on an uncontrolled slide down to the tunnel.

Princess Snowflake III began to help, blowing her fire on the icy rocks and clearing the way for Lachlan.

Together, we climbed slowly down the rocks as the air became colder. Soon, I could see my breath in front of my face. Every inch of me was freezing except for the part that was covered by my jacket. Whatever magic the Seamstress had imbued it with, it worked.

By the time we reached the bottom, I was shaking and exhausted. My hands were bloodied and aching, and my muscles screamed.

I turned to face the bottom level of Hell.

"It deserves its name." Lachlan's gaze was grim as he surveyed the terrain in front of us.

Slick blue ice covered the ground, looking like a deadly hockey ring. Whirling snow fell from the sky, carried on a biting wind.

"I would almost prefer a hell that is hot." I pulled up the collar of my jacket.

Not in Dante's Inferno. Muffin's gaze turned serious. *This is the part that I never come to. It's horrible.*

"That's the truth. Let's get a move on." I started forward, and Muffin took the hint.

He flew ahead, leading us across the icy terrain. *I'm not sure where the stone will be, but I have an idea.*

"Where?"

The worst part of hell, of course. Where the Devil resides.

Lachlan looked at me. "Translation?"

"He's leading us to the Devil."

"Literally?"

Literally. Muffin turned back, his green eyes glinting with warning. *But we must be very quiet. If we're lucky, we won't wake him.*

Oh, perfect.

Bojangles ran ahead of us, sliding over the ice. But even he didn't show his usual joy. Princess Snowflake III trudged along, her long fur blowing in the wind. She was so white that she nearly disappeared amongst the blowing snow.

We moved as fast as we could, racing across the icy ground. I tucked myself against Lachlan, his warmth protecting me from the howling wind. The snow was so strong that it stung where it hit my skin. The slick surface of the ground nearly made me fall a dozen times, but desperation helped me keep my footing, along with Lachlan's strong grip.

We couldn't afford an injury. Not now.

A crashing sounded from up ahead, and I looked at Muffin. "What's that?"

I don't know. I don't come down here enough, and the landscape is ever changing. But I bet a pound of tuna it's not crashing gold.

"No, I imagine not." I translated his words for Lachlan.

Finally, I caught sight of what was creating the noise. There was a massive ravine cutting straight through Hell. It stretched at least one hundred feet wide, blocking our way, and plunged down into the depths of the earth.

We stopped far from the edge, inspecting the skinny ice bridge that crossed the gash in the earth. A massive pendulum swung from the ceiling above, smashing into the bridge and breaking it into a million pieces. More ice formed, growing to recreate the bridge. But seconds later, the pendulum smashed it again.

"There's not enough time to get across." Lachlan's gaze was grim.

If only I could turn into the Battle Crow once again. I closed my eyes and tried, imagining myself as the huge black bird. I could almost feel the wind in my feathers.

But nothing happened. I didn't shift.

Believe.

The word played in my mind. Believe? In myself?

Risk.

Risk what?

"I can slow time just long enough to get across." Lachlan's words cut through my thoughts. "But we'll have to be fast. I can only do it for so long before time forces itself forward and I lose control."

I looked at him. "Do it."

I'd worry about the Battle Crow later. This was more reliable, and we were in a hurry. With the castle being attacked, there was no time for me to figure out my stuff.

Slowly, Lachlan approached the bridge, his hands raised as magic surged on the air. The forest scent of his power cut through the reek of death, the first relief that I'd had in this horrible place.

Lachlan's magic flowed from him, and I felt the air begin to change. Subtly at first, and then the pendulum creaked to a stop. It hung suspended in midair, a visceral threat.

Lachlan held out his hand. "Hold on. The path will be slippery. And we only get one shot."

I reached out and gripped his hand.

Bojangles led the way, sprinting across the slick surface of the skinny bridge. Princess Snowflake III followed, her stride quick and sure.

Muffin flew near my head, his green gaze on mine. *I'll keep you from falling.*

Somehow I doubted that he would be strong enough to keep me upright if I fell off the bridge, but I appreciated the thought. "Thanks, pal."

"Let's go." Lachlan led the way toward the bridge.

I didn't dare look down as I stepped onto the slippery surface. It was only eighteen inches across, so skinny that one misplaced footstep would send me hurtling over the edge and plummeting into the dark depths of hell.

My heart thundered as we began to cross. The ice was slick beneath my boots, and every footstep felt like it might be my last. My skin was so cold from the snow and fear that it had gone numb.

Keep it up! You're doing great! Muffin fluttered alongside me, his cheery voice totally at odds with our nightmare surroundings.

The wind plowed into us, nearly blowing me off my feet at times. Lachlan's warm grip felt like the only thing tethering me to the world.

"When this is all over, I'm never going near heights again."

But the dream flashed in my mind, bringing with it the image of me jumping off the cliff at the Protectorate castle.

I prayed it wasn't a premonition. I *really* didn't want to do that.

"We're almost there." Lachlan's voice was strong and sure. Heights didn't bother him, apparently.

I pretended that I had some of his bravery, and honestly, it kind of helped. Foot in front of foot, I kept going, focusing only on what was ahead of me.

We were almost to the edge when Lachlan's magic snapped. Time forced its way back to life, and the pendulum creaked.

It's coming! Muffin's panicked meow cut through the air.

Bojangles and Princess Snowflake III were already on the other side, and both of them turned their wide gazes to the pendulum behind me. They shrieked, their loud meows cutting through the air.

I glanced back at the pendulum in time to see it swinging toward the bridge. It would crush the slender ice structure in seconds.

"Go!" I screamed.

Lachlan gave up his careful pace and sprinted ahead.

I followed him, my heart thundering as I raced across the bridge. The ground was slick beneath my feet, and every footstep threatened to send me to my death.

We were only five feet from the edge when the pendulum slammed into the bridge. It shattered, falling out from beneath my feet. I gripped Lachlan's hand hard, and he jumped. His free hand gripped the side of the cliff, and he held on tight.

"Try to find a foothold!" Lachlan's voice echoed through the ravine.

I struggled to find a place on the wall that I could cling to. Muffin's paws pressed against my butt as he tried to push me up against the wall. It helped, if only a bit.

Lachlan grunted as he pulled us upward. I managed to find a handhold in the ice, and gave it everything I had, straining to pull myself up without letting go of Lachlan's hand. It got easier when I found a foothold, but my stomach still felt like it was going to jump out of my throat.

Together, we scrambled up the cliff face. It should have been impossible, but somehow we made it. At the top, we flopped against the flat surface of the ice and gasped.

I took only a second to catch my breath, and then I climbed to my feet. Lachlan joined me, his face grim.

"Let's go." We spoke the words in unison. If the situation hadn't been so dire, I might've smiled.

Together, the five of us hurried across the slick ice of hell. The wind continued to howl and the snow flew. But there was something else in the air here, a feeling that tugged at my chest.

"I think we're getting close." I squinted, trying to see through the howling snow, but it was impossible. There was nothing but whiteness ahead of me.

Lead the way. Muffin's meow cut through the howling wind. *In all this snow, I can't see where we're going. Can you feel it with your Druid sense?*

I closed my eyes and focused, begging my Druid sense to answer the question: *Where is the Doomsday Stone.* It could usually help me answer questions, and I hoped it could help me answer this one.

Something tugged in my chest, and I followed it, my Druid sense coming to life and helping us navigate through the snowy terrain. Hopefully this meant that the Fates hadn't beaten us to the stone.

The wind howled as we pressed onward.

When a scratching sound came from my right, I tilted my head, trying to hear it better. "Do you hear that?"

"There's something there." Lachlan squinted into the distance. "Can't see what it is."

Nothing good. Worry glinted in Muffin's green gaze. *Be ready.*

We picked up the pace, somehow managing not to fall. But the scratching noise didn't go away. Something was approaching. My heart thundered in my ears.

Princess Snowflake III hissed, her gaze glued on the distance. Bojangles arched his back, orange fur sticking up.

When the figures appeared through the snow, my heart dropped. There were dozens of them, each shaped like a giant crab made of ice.

They scuttled forward, becoming easier to see. They weren't crabs. Not exactly, at least. They were ten-legged beasts with giant fangs and horns. Their eyes glittered with blue fire, and they snapped their massive pincers.

Hell beasts! Muffin hissed.

I called upon my magic, digging deep to find the fire within me. It swelled out of my chest and ignited in my hand. I hurled the fireball at the nearest hell beast. It exploded against its glimmering blue form, and the creature blasted apart.

Lachlan hurled a jet of water at one of the hell beasts. At first, it seemed like a dumb idea. But it was so cold that the water froze in midair. By the time it hit the hell beast, it had become a spear. The weapon plowed into the creature and both shattered. Shards of ice flew in every direction.

"Nice," I said, continuing to throw my fire.

"I thought that might work." He threw another spear, achieving the same effect. "Glad I was right."

Together we hurled ice and fire at the monsters, taking out one after the other.

Princess Snowflake III charged, blasting her fiery breath at any creature that got in her way. She moved so quickly and so ferociously that she took out a dozen of them in less than a minute. Bojangles followed, plowing into them so hard that they broke into hundreds of pieces. Muffin did the same, attacking from the air and yowling his battle cry.

But there were so many of them! They kept coming, wave after wave. Dozens upon dozens. Never ending.

I looked at Lachlan. "This isn't working. They'll never stop coming."

"We need to outrun them." His magic swelled on the air, and a moment later, he shifted into his black lion form. I leapt onto his back, crouching low over his neck and hanging on to his wild mane.

"Cats! Retreat!"

Princess Snowflake III yowled as if she were pissed at being asked to leave her prey, but she did as I asked. We had to keep going, and she knew it. The cats raced toward us, joining us as Lachlan began to race away from the giant ice monsters.

I turned around, sending blasts of fire at them as we retreated. It held them off long enough that we could gain some distance. But they kept chasing us, their numbers continuing to grow.

We could keep our distance from them, but if they kept following us, we wouldn't be able to stop and retrieve the Doomsday Stone.

We had to get away from them, but how?

Up ahead! Muffins meowed.

I squinted through the howling snow, my eyes almost numb from the cold. I'd always thought eyes couldn't go numb, but in Hell, apparently anything was possible. It looked like there was a river up ahead, a brilliant blue rush of liquid that couldn't be water. It reeked of death and moved so quickly that it would wash us away if we stepped into it.

"Can you jump it?" I gripped Lachlan's mane tighter.

He roared, and I took it to be a confirmation.

"Cats, get on!" They could run as fast as Lachlan, but could they jump that far?

Princess Snowflake III and Bojangles leapt onto Lachlan's back, and I grabbed them both, holding them tight to my chest. Lachlan picked up the pace as he neared the river, seeming to give it every ounce of energy he had. He'd never gone so fast. We were almost there when he jumped, his powerful legs carrying us into the air.

I crouched low over his back, clutching the cats tightly.

You're going to make it! Muffin flew alongside us.

I prayed he was right. The water below was rushing by at a hundred miles an hour at least. We'd never survive if we fell in.

Lachlan landed on the other side of the river and kept running. I turned around, watching as the ice monsters raced into the water. It swept them away, carrying them off into the darkness.

"They're gone." My Druid sense still tugged at my chest. We were close. "Slow down. Stop."

Lachlan slowed to a halt, and I climbed off, the cats jumping out of my arms. Princess Snowflake III shook herself as if I'd been dirty, and I grinned.

Magic surged on the air as Lachlan shifted back into his human form. He raked a hand through his dark hair. "That was close."

I gave a breathless laugh, nerves and shock making me giddy. "No kidding. We're almost there. Let's go."

I led us through the howling wind and snow. In the distance, a massive mountain rose out of the ground. It was oddly shaped, lumpy and bigger on one side than the other.

Muffin slowed and looked at me. *That's the Devil.*

Confusion raced through me, and I squinted at the mountain. It was closer than I realized, more of a giant hill than a mountain.

It really *was* the Devil. He was frozen, half in the ice and half out of it. His upper body crouched over itself, his black wings folded over his back.

A sense of evil flowed out from him, so great that it made my insides feel like they were coated in black oil. If I stayed near him long enough, it would taint me, too. I would become as evil as he was.

I'd never felt magic as black as that. There was nothing in Darklane or The Vaults that could compare to this. Even the Fates weren't that evil.

Lachlan reached for my hand and squeezed. I drew from his strength, grateful for the warmth.

"Let's be quick." His voice was so low that I could barely hear it.

I nodded, and we started forward. Even Bojangles crept along, the cat who never censored himself or went quiet was now as silent as the grave.

My Druid sense tugged us toward the Devil's front side. Up close, it was clear that he was sleeping. My heart thundered in my ears, so loud that I was surprised he didn't wake. He was at least one hundred feet tall, and that was only his upper half. The rest of him was buried deep below the ice.

Why?

I didn't have time to dwell. My Druid sense led me to the space right in front of the Devil. His head was bowed over us, a face of pure cruelty and evil, even in repose.

I pointed toward a spot in the ice, not daring to speak. We approached it, and every step made my Druid sense tug harder. It rarely worked, and I was grateful that it was leading us toward our target now. It had to be here. It had to.

I hated the idea of the castle under attack, and we needed to get there before the wall fell. I didn't know how much Seawort my sisters had been able to find, or how much potion they had been able to make, but I'd bet that there were unprotected members of the Protectorate who would become the Fates' slaves as soon as the castle wall fell.

I knelt on the ice, peering into it. There was a faint blue light encapsulated entirely in the solid frozen water. It was a few feet down, from the looks of it, totally trapped.

It's here.

We'd beaten them.

We had to melt the ice.

As if he knew what needed to be done, Lachlan stood guard over me, his gaze riveted to the Devil, watching for any movement. I turned my attention to the ice, and hovered my hand directly over it. I called upon my magic, letting it rise inside of me. I directed the flame toward the ice. It glowed bright, beginning to melt the frozen water.

Princess Snowflake III approached and sat next to me. She blew her own fire on the ice, helping me melt the protective casing that surrounded the Doomsday Stone.

Together, we melted the stone's cage. Meltwater formed a pool. By the time we melted the ice all the way to the stone, weakness dragged at me. I stopped as soon as I could, and stared into the water. The Doomsday Stone was about two and a half feet inside. I reached my hand into the cold water, wincing as it closed around my limb. Icicles of pain stabbed me, but I resisted, thrusting my arm deeper.

My palm closed around the stone, and magic shot up my arm. I yanked it out of the water and stared at it.

Dread opened a hole in my chest.

The stone was broken in half.

Maybe it had always looked like this, but I seriously doubted it. The stone had obviously been split in two and was missing the other side. I looked up and met Lachlan's gaze. Concern creased his brow, and he clearly thought the same thing.

Someone had gotten here before us. I didn't know when, but they'd taken half the stone.

The Fates.

"Well, well. I am surprised that you made it this far."

I leapt to my feet, shock racing through me. I spun, looking for the owner of the voice.

A man strolled toward us, someone that I had never seen before. He had a long narrow face with a hooked nose and small mouth. His red robes looked ancient. A circle of leaves sat upon his head, each dripping with icicles.

"Dante Alighieri?" Lachlan asked.

The man nodded. "Yes, how did you know?"

"I read your book, and I've seen paintings of you. You have a distinct face."

Dante's grin spread wide. "Yes, I am immortal."

"Why are you here?" I asked.

"This is my realm." He swept his arms wide, indicating the frozen wasteland that surrounded us. "Are you not impressed?"

Yeah, Arach had been right. Dante really wasn't right in the head. But I couldn't worry about that now.

I held up the stone. "Why is there only half of the stone? Did the Fates get here before us?"

"Long ago, when I was still alive and able to walk the earth, I took it to the Protectorate castle." He grinned, clearly delighted to tell us a story. "A seer had told me that it would be hunted. It was encapsulated in the ice, and I could only break off half of it." Envy glinted in his eyes. "If I had your gift of fire, perhaps I could've melted the ice and taken the entire stone. You must be very strong if you can melt this ice. It is stronger than any rock on earth."

I looked at Princess Snowflake III, and she grinned, her fangs glinting.

"But it was fine. I only needed half the stone," he continued.

"You were trying to protect the stone?" Suspicion sounded in Lachlan's voice.

"But of course." Dante gave a strange smile, and a shiver raced down my spine.

"But that doesn't protect it." I frowned at him. "The Elders of the Indomidae said that the stone is so powerful that you can use it even if you only have a piece."

Dante grinned even wider. "Precisely."

Horror filled me. "You weren't helping the Protectorate. You were helping the Fates. You were splitting the stone so that it would be harder for us to destroy it. But they could still use one piece of it."

Arach had said there were rumors he wasn't right in the head. This proved it.

"Yes. I didn't know where else to hide it, so I took it to the castle, the safest place in the world. I knew the Fates would need it one day because they came to me and told me in a dream. This plan has been in place for hundreds of years. And now it is finally coming to fruition." He laughed. "The stone can't be destroyed unless two parts are together. You're too late!"

That's why they were attacking the castle now. Not just to break the walls, but also to get the stone. They never even needed to come to hell. That's why we hadn't seen them on our journey here.

They had what they needed inside the castle walls. The stone would make their curse permanent. They'd enslave our friends. Forever.

"But why would you help the Fates?" I just couldn't wrap my mind around it.

Dante swept his hands out to indicate hell. "Because they allowed me to spend eternity here, of course, and made me a King of Hell. They modified my fate, and in return, I helped them."

He really *was* obsessed with hell.

"And you must admit, the Doomsday Spell is quite tantalizing." His eyes gleamed with the light of insanity.

Oh man, I really hadn't seen this coming.

"Where is the stone in the castle?" Lachlan asked.

My heart thundered in my ears. I could call my sisters and tell them where it was.

Dante shook his head. "Alas, our time together is over. Just as this life is over for you."

He looked at the Devil, and I knew what he would do. Fear iced in my chest.

"Wake!" he shouted, so loudly that my eardrums felt like they were bleeding. "Rise, oh cursed one!"

I looked at Lachlan as my heart began to pound. "Run."

Follow me! Muffin flew away.

Princess Snowflake III and Bojangles sprinted after him, so fast that they were blurs in the snow. Dante's shouts echoed around us.

I shoved the stone into my pocket. Lachlan and I raced away from the Devil as the earth began to creak and groan. The Devil was breaking free, and he was *mad.*

14

The ice exploded behind us as the Devil's bellow rent the silence of the snowy night. I glanced behind us and spotted the Devil climbing out of the ice, rising to his full height. He towered two hundred feet tall, his massive black wings spreading out behind him. He swept them backward, and the wind that he created blasted the snow away from him.

Dante cackled like a maniac. But then, clearly, he was. Anyone who willingly lived in hell was a crazy person.

The Devil's red gaze met my own, and he opened his mouth on a wide, eerie grin, his fangs glinting. I turned away and ran faster. The Devil's pounding footsteps sounded behind us, shaking the earth so much that my legs trembled and I nearly lost my footing.

"Where's the exit?" Lachlan shouted.

Up ahead! Muffin flew faster. *Not far now.*

I translated for Lachlan, gasping for breath as I ran. I'd run from some scary things in my life, but nothing as scary as the Devil himself. The cats sprinted like the hounds of hell were on their tails, and they weren't far off.

"We're not fast enough." Lachlan's magic surged on the air as he shifted into his black lion form, never breaking stride.

I leapt upon his back and clung to his mane. I used the opportunity to turn around and look at the Devil.

He was gaining on us, his strides so enormous that he would be on us in two steps. In the distance, Dante Alighieri stood, laughing as his red robes blew around his legs.

I threw a blast of flame at the Devil, but he just absorbed it and laughed.

Okay, new plan.

I tried wind next, but it had no effect on a figure as big as the Devil. I might have blown a golden rock out of the sky, but he was too big.

He reached us, raising his foot to stomp us into the ground.

"Left!" I screamed.

Lachlan darted left, so strong and quick that he managed to avoid the Devil's attack.

The enormous foot slammed into the ice, cracking it deeply. Lachlan leapt over one of the cracks, darting around another. The Cats of Catastrophe led the way through the snow, their steps swift and sure. We followed them, desperately dodging the Devil's footsteps as he chased us through the snowy wasteland of hell.

Almost there! Muffin darted left, and we followed.

I turned to look up at the Devil, his black magic nearly flattening me into the ground. He was so dark that he had to be the opposite of me. I called upon the light within me, shining it toward him. The golden glow blasted out from me and struck him in the chest. He lurched backward, but quickly regained his strength, surging forward and racing after us.

Get ready to jump!

I hit the Devil with my light again, buying us a few extra seconds.

We're here! Muffin flew straight into a black hole in the ground, and the other cats wasted no time in following.

Lachlan leapt in after them. I clung to his mane as we fell, looking back in time to see the Devil's angry face as he watched us disappear.

The ether sucked us in and spat us out at the top of Mount Vesuvius. The sun hovered near the horizon, lighting the volcano in a golden glow. My heart thundered as I slid off of Lachlan, my legs so weak that I nearly fell.

Holy tuna, that was close. Muffin turned to look at me, his green eyes sharp. *Did you get the rock?*

Princess Snowflake III gave me a look that said I had better have gotten the rock. Bojangles seemed to have already forgotten about our disastrous adventure and was chasing moths around the rocks.

"I've got it." I gripped it tight in my palm. "We need to get back to the castle."

Magic crackled around my comms charm. As if she'd heard my words, Bree's voice echoed through. "They've broken through the wall! The demons are spilling into the courtyard."

My terrified gaze met Lachlan's. "They're in."

That meant that the castle's magical defenses had fallen. My friends were now slaves to the Fates. Anyone who had a tattoo but had not taken the protective Seawort potion would be susceptible to the Fates' control. How much Seawort had Bree and Rowan managed to find? I hoped it was enough. I needed time to destroy the entire Doomsday Stone before the Fates found it. Otherwise, their spell would become permanent.

"Can you make us a portal?" I asked Lachlan.

His magic was already flaring on the air, and the portal was forming. "Go."

I followed his command, stepping through the portal alongside the Cats of Catastrophe. Once again, the ether sucked me in. This time, it spat me out into chaos.

I stood on the castle lawn as a battle raged about one hundred yards away. There was a massive break in the exterior wall, close to the sea. The Fates' demon forces had broken through and were spilling onto the castle grounds. Dozens of them were already on the courtyard, fighting my friends and allies. I watched with horror as Ali and Haris fought against other members of the Protectorate.

They must not have gotten any of the Seawort potion. They were now slaves to the Fates.

Horror spread through me like tar. Lachlan appeared next to me.

I looked at him, barely able to speak.

"We're too late." My voice was nothing more than a croak.

"Ana!" Bree's voice sounded from the sky, and I looked up.

She flew down to meet us and landed gracefully on the ground, her silver wings flaring behind her. "They broke through three minutes ago. There was a spot in the castle wall that was still weak from the damage done months ago when the fae portal nearly destroyed the castle. We didn't realize it was there, but they found it. They've almost overrun our forces."

"How many are on their side? How many of our friends have they turned?"

"We only had enough Seawort potion for half. The rest became the Fates' slaves as soon as the wall fell and the castle's protections disappeared."

Oh no. Half of our forces were against us. Half of them turned. If the Fates got to the Doomsday Stone before me, they could enslave those of us who had taken the Seawort potion as well. The protection of the potion was temporary, but we needed every minute we could get to break the curse.

Or we'd all be their slaves, unable to fight back.

I'd be their slave.

Forever.

I spun in a circle, taking in the fight around me. It was a catastrophe. Demons everywhere. Protectorate members were fighting Protectorate members. Those who had already been enslaved were able to use their magic against their friends who were still protected by the Seawort potion. I spotted several people, dead on the ground.

My friends. My colleagues.

My heart thundered, fear and panic creating a noxious stew in my stomach.

This couldn't be.

It was too terrible to be real.

I had to fix it.

I *could* fix it.

I was the Morrigan. I could change fate.

I didn't know where the two Fates were, but I had to turn back time to get us on an even footing. To save the lives that had already been lost. Only then could I begin my hunt for the other half of the Doomsday Stone. But I needed time to find it, and the only way to get that time was to turn back the clock and evict the demons from the castle.

But how? My gaze was drawn to the break in the castle wall. That was where the damage had been done. I couldn't change much without risk, but I could change that moment.

I hadn't practiced this and I didn't know exactly how I would do it, but I felt it deep in my soul. It was possible.

I needed to get to the wall, but there were dozens of demon forces between me and my goal. Running was too dangerous, but the buggy could get us there.

I looked at Bree. "I need to get to the break in the castle wall. Where's the buggy?"

"Hang on a second." Bree passed her fingers to her comms charm and shot into the air, racing away toward the castle.

Lachlan looked at me. "What are you thinking?"

"I have to become the Morrigan." I still had to figure out how I would do that exactly, but first, I needed to get to the break in the castle wall.

A moment later, the buggy came careening through the crowd of demons, racing toward us. Bree flew above, directing Rowan as she drove the buggy. Caro stood on the front platform, firing arrows at oncoming demons. Fortunately, she was still protected by the Seawort potion.

Unfortunately, that meant she wasn't in control of her magic. She was good with the bow and arrow, though, taking out demon after demon who blocked their way.

"Do you have it?" Rowan screamed as she pulled the buggy to a stop in front of me. "Do you have the Doomsday Stone?"

"Half of it. But there's something I have to do first." I needed to turn back time to save those who were already lost. And we needed an advantage. We couldn't win like this, not if they were already within the castle walls.

Rowan frowned at my mention of half the stone, but shouted, "Then get in!"

I climbed onto the front platform, taking a position next to Caro. Lachlan climbed on the back. The Cats of Catastrophe raced off into the fight.

Rowan stepped on the gas, and the buggy jumped forward, surging toward the horde of demons that were still flowing through the castle wall. We'd have to fight our way through them to get to the hole in the wall.

Caro fired her arrows, taking out an endless stream of demons. I chose fire, lighting them up like barbecues. Screams rent the air, but I felt no guilt. They were here to enslave my family and destroy my home.

I would do whatever it took.

Bree's lightning struck from the sky, while Lachlan heaved at the earth, making the demons lose their footing and fall beneath the pounding footsteps of their companions. They were crushed underneath the horde.

As Rowan drove like a maniac, I searched for the Fates. Were they already inside, hunting for the second half of the Doomsday Stone? They might even know where it was hidden if Dante had told them.

I turned to look at the castle, catching sight of the Fates running through the massive front doors.

Dread filled me. We would have to be fast. If they got to the stone first, the curse would be permanent. I didn't even know if my Morrigan powers could turn back time.

"Faster!" I turned to face forward, watching us approach the wall.

Rowan steered the buggy around demons, driving straight over their corpses if they got in the way. By the time we reached the hole in the castle wall, they had all run through, invading the castle grounds. It was quiet here, the remains of our defenses in pieces.

I climbed out of the buggy and inspected the damage.

I had to turn back time here, just like I had with the seal woman.

My friends watched me silently, confusion on their faces. I ignored them, closing my eyes and focusing on the magic within me.

I didn't know what I was looking for, but it had to be inside me. I was the Morrigan, right? I had shifted into the Battle Crow, proving it to be true. The Elders had helped me jumpstart my fate powers before, but this time I had to do it alone. I had to fully transform into a Dragon God to become the Morrigan.

But no matter how hard I searched, I couldn't find a way to

change fate. It was easy to find my earth magic, or my light magic. All of those were so easy now.

But I couldn't see the molecules of time like I had before. Just thinking it sounded insane.

There was something I was missing.

My gaze was drawn to the cliff that plunged into the sea. The dream flashed in my mind's eye.

Believe.

Risk.

I knew what I had to do. I didn't hesitate. I didn't stop. I didn't think.

I just ran.

I sprinted for the cliff, running as fast as I ever had. My friends' screams sounded from behind me, but I ignored them.

I had to believe in myself. I had to risk it all.

In the dream, I had jumped off the cliff and turned into the Battle Crow.

I had to do that now. It *had* been a premonition.

And I couldn't give myself time to doubt. I was too afraid of heights to stop and doubt.

Bree appeared above me, flying fast with her silver wings. "No! Ana, no!"

"Don't try to catch me!" I ran faster, my heart thundering. I couldn't focus on my fear. There was too much at stake to spend time on worry. If I couldn't turn back time, the Protectorate was gone. My friends enslaved. And eventually, the Fates could destroy the world with their new army of the unwilling.

I reached the edge of the cliff and jumped.

For the briefest second, fear pierced my heart. It was impossible not to feel it when the ground fell out from under me and I plummeted toward the sea. The wind tore at my hair and made my eyes water, and my stomach pitched.

But I was the Morrigan.

I was the Battle Crow.

Magic swelled inside my chest, something greater and brighter than I had ever experienced. It felt like the sun rising inside me, pushing out all the dark spaces and weaknesses and fears. My power grew exponentially. It was a living thing that I could feel, filling me up and making me whole.

Suddenly, the wind caught beneath my wings. I swept up on a current of air, leaving the surface of the sea behind. I had shifted.

I had risked, and it had worked!

I was the Battle Crow. The Morrigan. A full Dragon God.

Joy surged in my chest as the wind blew through my feathers. I rose high in the air and turned, my new and stronger vision easily finding my friends standing near the break in the castle wall.

Shock painted their features as they looked at me, and I swept in a circle over the castle grounds, inspecting the damage.

Hordes of demons were surrounding the main castle building. They fought my friends, sending fire and ice and wind and steel through the crowds of people. Though my friends fought bravely, they were overwhelmed. It tore at my heart to see Protectorate members fighting their friends and colleagues. Those who were already enslaved had looks of such torture on their faces that I couldn't bear it. They were being forced by those they loved.

Hatred for the Fates swelled in my chest. I would do whatever it took to stop them.

I turned from the site of the battle, the image of my friends' falling bodies burned into my mind.

I flew back to the break in the castle wall and focused on it.

Not only was my vision stronger, but it was easier to see the way that time was part of the air. It looked just like when I'd been with the seal woman and changed her fate.

I had to do the same thing here.

I reached out with my magic and grasped time. It was easier now, though I still didn't understand the physics of how I did it. But perhaps I wasn't supposed to. That's why it was magic.

The power of the Morrigan flowed through me. I was a conduit for the magic that began to twist the molecules in the air, turning back time slowly and completely.

The battle went silent. The whole *world* went silent.

I turned to look at the fighters. They had stopped, and the demons were walking backward toward the break in the castle wall. It was as if I were watching a movie on rewind. This was so much bigger than it had been with the seal woman. So many more people and so much more damage to fix. But I pushed my magic hard, making it happen. I never could have done this as a half Dragon God. The demons flowed back to the castle wall, a horde of them disappearing from the grounds. Even the Fates were sucked back out of the castle and across the lawn toward the break in the wall.

They looked up at me, somehow able to break through the freezing power of my magic. Rage lit their faces.

But I was too strong. I continued to turn back time, dragging all of the demons out of the castle. When every last one was out of the grounds, the wall began to rebuild itself. I pushed my magic a little bit farther, giving us just a bit of time before the castle wall broke again. But I couldn't go back too far, or I would risk too much. I could only change fate in the smallest way.

I let the spell stop.

Sound returned to the world. My friends were shouting below as they prepared for the invasion. Some stood on the castle walls, attacking the forces that had gathered outside. But no one seemed to notice that the wall was weak at the base. I looked around, searching for the buggy and my sisters.

Searching for Lachlan. They were no longer where I had left them because I had turned back time.

I hoped that I hadn't gone too far back. If I was *here* at the same time I should be in hell, taking the Doomsday Stone, then perhaps I would never take the stone at all. I flew back to the ground, shifting into human form as my feet landed on the earth. I plunged my hand into my pocket, grateful to find that the stone was still there. Thank fates I hadn't gone back too far.

I looked toward the castle, to the space where Lachlan and I had appeared when we'd arrived. I had to wait a few moments for time to catch up, then he appeared, along with the Cats of Catastrophe. Shock flashed in his eyes when he realized that I wasn't next to him.

I waved my arms at him, gesturing him closer.

Confusion streaked across his face, then he loped toward me.

As he approached, I pressed my fingertips to the comms charm at my throat. "Bree! Rowan! Where are you? I'm here, near the eastern part of the wall. Come meet me."

"We'll be there," Bree's voice echoed from the charm.

Lachlan joined me. I pointed to the part of the castle wall that would soon break. "We have to pile the earth up in front of the wall there, reinforcing it."

"Okay." He looked at me, questions in his eyes. "Then later, we can discuss how you disappeared suddenly."

"No problem. This first, that second." None of my friends had experienced what I had just experienced. I had changed fate, and I was the only one with the memory of the battle.

It was for the best. The misery on my friends' faces as they fought each other was enough to haunt me forever. I was glad they didn't have to live with it.

Lachlan and I faced the castle wall, each of us digging deep for our magic. I called upon the earth, forcing it to rise up and mound against the back of the castle wall. It provided extra rein-forcement, and I kept going, piling tons upon tons of dirt against the wall.

I just prayed it would be enough, because this fight was a long way from over.

15

I finished shoving the dirt against the wall just as Bree landed next to me, her gaze confused.

A second later, Rowan drove up in the buggy. Caro still rode on the front, but this time, Jude had joined her. No doubt she'd hitched a ride to come see what was going on with the dirt against the wall. The three FireSouls were nearby as well. Cass, Del, and Nix all ran up, questions on their faces.

"What's going on?" Jude asked.

I pointed to the pile of dirt against the wall. "That section of the wall is still weak from the damage caused by the fae portal months ago. The Fates broke through it fifteen minutes ago, but I turned back time and changed fate."

Shock flashed across everyone's faces.

Nix frowned, her green eyes confused. "That should be impossible."

"Ten minutes ago, it was. But it turns out that I'm the Morrigan, and I can change fate. At least a little bit."

Everyone's brows rose.

"Wow, you're mega powerful." Del, her dark hair glinting in the sun, nodded approvingly. "That's some magic to come into."

"I'm not sure if I have enough magic to do it again, so we have to defend that part of the wall. If it breaks, we're lost."

Cade, Bree's boyfriend, arrived as soon as I said the words. His dark eyes traveled from mine to Jude's. "I'll lead the forces and get started on the defense."

Jude nodded. "Excellent. Thank you, Cade."

He pulled Bree close and pressed a quick kiss to her cheek. "Be careful."

She met his gaze. "You too."

He loped off toward the wall, calling out to Ali and Haris as he ran, asking them to help gather the forces.

"What else?" Rowan's gaze met mine. "You look like there's something else."

"Did you find the stone?" Jude asked.

"I found half of it, but I still have to find the rest. It was broken and stolen centuries ago and hidden somewhere in the castle."

"I'll help," Cass said. She stepped forward, her red hair glinting in the sun, her brown leather jacket protecting her from the worst of the winter cold.

"Thanks." Her dragon sense was more reliable than my Druid sense. I might be able to find the stone, but together, our odds were so much better. And I was never dumb enough to turn down help. I dug into my pocket and held out the stone. It was about the size of my palm with one jagged edge.

Cass hovered her hand over the stone and closed her eyes. Her magic swelled on the air. Her eyes popped open. "Definitely in the castle. Far below the main structure."

"That makes sense." Jude's starry blue eyes sharpened. "It's the only place where we wouldn't have found it until now. Who put it there?"

"Dante Alighieri," Lachlan said. "He's been working against you all this time. On the side of the Fates."

A shadow passed across Jude's face. "That bastard."

"We won't let his plan succeed." Anger surged in my chest at the memory of his betrayal. "Let's go get this damned stone."

Del stepped forward. "Nix and I will go defend the wall. If you need help, just call."

"Be careful," Cass said.

"You too." Nix hugged her, then turned and ran off toward the wall with Del.

"Rowan and I can help them," Bree said. "Good luck, Ana."

I reached out and grabbed her arm. "No, come with me. I think I'm going to need you. I can just feel it."

Jude nodded. "The five of you go find the stone. The rest of us will defend the walls."

"Hold them off as long as you can. We need all the time we can get." Failure was not an option.

Jude nodded, then turned and strode toward the castle wall.

"Let's go." I sprinted toward the castle, the others at my side.

We passed dozens of our friends, all of whom were carrying more weapons from the armory. Hundreds of bows and arrows, dozens of potion bombs. So few of us had our magic that we needed all the weapons we could get. We sprinted across the courtyard and ran up into the main entry hall of the castle.

"Let's head to the library." I turned toward it. "If the stone is deep underground, it's probably in that cavern that is accessed through the stairs in the ghost library."

As quickly as we could, we ran down the hall toward the library. As soon as we entered, Florian drifted through the wall. He didn't even bother announcing his presence with his usual wail. The librarian's face was pale, even for a ghost. His fancy wig sat askew on his head, the curls going every which way.

"Are you okay?" Florian wrung his hands. "How is the battle going? It sounds like it's terrible."

"We need to get underneath the castle." I ran past him, and

he followed, drifting along. "Do you know of any unfamiliar stones down there, any unfamiliar magic or something out of the ordinary?"

He shook his head. "No, nothing seems different than it ever has."

"The stone would have been put there before your time here," Lachlan said. "I don't think that anything would feel different to you."

"Well then, I will help you look." He nodded, determined.

"Great, we can use all the help we can get." I sprinted toward the ghost library, slipping through the small door at the side of the bookshelves and stepping onto the wide platform that overlooked the cavernous space.

"Whoa." Cass breathed the word. "This place is amazing. Del would die to get in here."

I had to assume that Del liked books. That, or dust motes, because there were about one million of those, too.

Fortunately, the stairs appeared in front of us, leading us down to the next level.

"Thanks fates for that," Bree said. "We don't exactly have time to prove our worthiness here."

We sprinted down the stairs, cutting around the bookshelves and down the corridors, running until we reached the trapdoor that was set into the wooden floor. Lachlan pulled up the heavy door, and we ran down the narrow staircase, deeper into the darkness.

How much more time did we have? Had the wall fallen yet?

My heart thundered as we ran, worry filling my chest like an inflating balloon. I pushed it aside, trying to focus only on my goal.

The ancient stone staircase went far underground. As we went deeper, a blue light glowed brighter from below. A minute later, we spilled out into the cavernous space beneath the library. Glittery blue lights dripped from the ceiling, high-lighting the small lake in the middle of the cavern. The pedestal that sat on the little island in the middle contained the stone heart that held part of Arach's soul.

My gaze moved toward the tunnel that the Fates had dug into this cavern last month in order to steal Arach's stone heart. It was closed up and reinforced with extra protective magic. Thank fates it was still inaccessible. Ever since the break-in, we made a point to lock this place down tight. The result was that they were trying to break in through the castle walls rather than underground, but hopefully our forces could hold them off.

"Okay, everyone, spread out and look for a place where the stone could be hidden. It should be very subtle, since we searched this area last month." I started to search the empty space, sticking to the edges of the walls and hoping that my eyes might find something they hadn't before. My Druid sense tugged gently, but not enough to locate the stone. It was here, but I couldn't tell where, exactly. I looked at Cass. "Do you feel it?"

"The sensation is very diffuse. Some strange magic is blocking it."

I frowned, trying to focus on my Druid sense as I looked for the stone.

"They must have tried to steal it when they were here before," Bree said. "Thank fates they failed."

A minute later, my Druid sense tugged a bit harder. I followed it until my eye caught on something. I knelt down and squinted at the scratches in the stone. "I think I found something!"

Cass and the others hurried over.

"Do you think it's in there?" I asked Cass. My Druid sense tugged lightly, but I couldn't be sure. Magic was probably protecting it, just like Cass had said.

"I'd bet my trove on it," Cass said.

"No wonder these were missed before," Bree said.

Lachlan crouched down to inspect the scratches. "At least they didn't get far into the stone."

"Definitely not. I can feel the stone back there," Cass said.

I could feel it, too, though just barely.

"How do we get to the stone?" Bree asked.

"It's impossible." The powerful voice sounded from behind us, and I turned to see Arach standing there. "That is sealed against any but a dragon. I can feel something unfamiliar behind the rock wall, perhaps the stone you seek. But over time, this cavern has grown out to surround it."

"That's the castle's way of protecting us, isn't it?" I asked.

Arach nodded. "I heard what you said about Dante Alighieri. About how he betrayed the Protectorate. I didn't realize that he put the stone down here, but if a foreign object of great power was placed in the cavern, then the natural magic of this place would've ignited, enclosed around the object. Dante wouldn't have realized that, though. It is dragon lore."

Wow, that was amazing. The castle was like a living thing, protecting us the way that we protected it.

"You're a dragon," Bree said. "Can you help us?"

"I can. At least, I can try. Step aside."

We did as she asked, watching in awe as she shifted into the form of a true dragon. Magic swirled around her as her humanoid form grew and morphed. A moment later, a dragon stood in her place. Pale white and transparent, she was the size of a small house, with a graceful neck and powerful claws. She leaned forward, stretching out her neck and blasting her fire at the stone. The flame glowed a brilliant blue, and the stone began to melt away.

I stepped back, the heat almost more than I could bear. Awe filled my chest as I watched her.

"I don't know how the Fates expected to get to that stone without Arach," Rowan said.

"I'm sure they had a way." I no longer doubted the Fates. They could accomplish whatever they set out to do. To defeat them, we would have to be at our best.

Deep within Arach's flame, something glowed bright. She stepped back, cutting off her fire. A tiny black cave had formed, and the stone sat within, glowing brightly.

I hurried forward, entering the warm cave.

"Careful, that stone could be hot," Lachlan said.

I touched it carefully with a fingertip, and he was right. Blazing hot.

Maybe I didn't even need to pick it up. All I needed to do was destroy it. I wasn't sure yet how I would do that, but I had an idea.

I dug into my pocket and removed my half of the stone, then placed it against the broken side of the other stone. They fused together, flashing a bright white light.

The light confirmed that my idea might work. I stepped back. "I think I might know how to destroy the stone."

I called upon the magic within me, focusing on the light power that Sulis had given me. The light was good, and the stone was evil. Hopefully one could destroy the other. I directed my magic at the stone, giving it all that I had.

The white light glowed out of me, shooting toward the stone and making it shine a brilliant white.

The air vibrated with dark magic, and something burst from the stone.

A shadowy demon! The figure was about my size, but semi-transparent and gray. Massive horns rose from its head, and it charged me.

The Doomsday Stone was fighting back. Somehow, it'd been

imbued with a protective charm that made demons burst from it.

Bree intercepted the demon who hurtled toward me, swinging her sword for its neck. The blade collided, and the demon exploded in a poof of dust.

Another demon burst out of the stone, and another. My friends engaged the attackers as I kept sending my light into the stone. Cass destroyed one demon with a fire ball, while Rowan hit another with her dagger. Lachlan used his sword, slicing through the middle of a demon with such speed that I could barely see the blade.

I suddenly understood why I'd felt compelled to ask them to come with me.

"Keep going!" Lachlan shouted. "We've got your back."

As they fought, I reached deep for every ounce of magic that was in my soul. It poured out of me, stronger than ever. Only the light could destroy the Doomsday Stone.

I just had to be strong enough.

It took everything that I had to stay on my feet as I poured my power into the stone. I kept going until I could see nothing but the bright white glow of Sulis's light of life. I could hear the fighting around me, but saw none of it. It shot toward the stone, bowling out of me like a freight train. An explosion blasted from the cave, and we were thrown back. I skidded against the dirt, colliding with my friends.

When the rubble settled, I rose to my feet, my heart thundering. We were lucky that the whole place hadn't come down around us.

I'd blown a hole in the side of the cave that was the size of a car. There was no stone within the cave, and all the demons were gone. There was no stone anywhere, in fact.

I turned to everyone else. "I think we did it."

"You destroyed the Doomsday Stone." Arach's voice echoed with authority. "I can feel that it is no longer here."

We'd done it. The spell would never be permanent. But we still needed to defeat the Fates and save our friends. The battle was raging outside, and the demon forces were strong.

"Let's go finish this fight," I said.

We sprinted out of the cavern, climbing stairs as fast as we could and racing through the library. The sound of battle greeted us as we ran outside. All of our forces were gathered near the castle wall, launching an attack against the demons outside.

We sprinted toward them, climbing up onto the wall. I joined Connor, the potion maker from Magic's Bend. He was hurling potion bombs at the demons at the base of the wall. All around, Protectorate members fired arrows and potion bombs at the enemy. The few who had any magic left used it, but there weren't many.

There were hundreds of demons outside the wall. Dozens of them slammed huge battering rams into the castle wall, shaking it beneath our feet.

I scanned the crowd for the Fates, finally spotting them near the back. They were surrounded by their demon warriors, a bodyguard troop of hundreds.

"We need to figure out how to get to them." I frowned. But how? Their troops would destroy us before we even got close. "If I can get close, I can destroy them with my light."

"We can try launching an attack from the sky." Bree looked up. "But there are enough of them that control fire and ice that we would be in trouble."

"No, we have to take out most of the demons, or cause a big enough distraction that we can get to the Fates without them attacking us." Lachlan inspected the demon hordes, looking for a weakness.

"I think I have something that might help." Connor dug into his sack of potions and pulled out a rock. "It's a special bomb. It uses the energy of the earth to disrupt the ground and make it explode upward."

Another super magical object disguised as a rock. I could use less of these in my life.

"I can disrupt the ground." Why hadn't I thought about that?

"Can you disrupt an area the size of a football field?" Connor asked.

"No, that's a bit big." Even with Lachlan's help, I couldn't manage that. "Your rock can do that?"

Connor grinned. "Yep. This will take out a *lot* of those demons, but we haven't been able to use it yet because we can't deploy it."

"How do we deploy it?" Lachlan asked.

"You need to put it on the ground and give it at least ten seconds in order for the stone's roots to make a connection with the earth. But you can't throw it or the magic will be disrupted. You have to place it down gently." He shrugged. "It's a work in progress and finicky, but I think it will do what you want."

"I know how to deliver the stone," Rowan said.

I looked at her. "The buggy?"

"Exactly."

"I like how you think," Bree said. "I'll help clear the way."

"Excellent. We'll deliver the stone right to the middle of them and then get out before it detonates." I looked at Connor. "How long do we have before that happens?"

"Not more than thirty seconds."

I turned to my sisters. "We'll have to be fast."

Connor gave me the stone. "My aim is good. I'll try to clear the path in front of the buggy. Everyone on the wall will. We'll distract them while you put the bomb in place."

"Thank you."

We sprinted from the wall, heading toward the buggy that Rowen had left parked in the middle of the castle grounds. Cade joined us, sprinting to catch up. Del and Nix followed, leaping into the middle seats of the Buggy.

"You're headed out into the demons, right?" Del asked.

"Yep." I took the front platform along with Lachlan, and Cass joined us.

"Excellent," Nix said. "Right into the action."

Rowan stepped on the gas, and the buggy leapt forward.

She drove straight for the gate, and shouted for it to open.

Hans's head peeked out from the gatehouse, and his wide eyes met ours. "I've got it!"

He scrambled to open the gate and pressed his hand to the heavy wood. The magic ignited and the gate disappeared. Rowan drove through, out into the open countryside. She took a left, gunning for the crowd of demons.

As we neared, I began to throw fire at the demons. The blasts lit them up like fireworks, and I threw as many as I could.

"I'm more useful from the ground." Lachlan pulled me close and gave me one fast kiss, then leapt off the buggy. He transformed into a lion before he hit the ground.

Cade followed him, shifting into the form of a huge gray wolf.

Del leapt out of the buggy and adopted her phantom form. She danced through the demons, her transparent blue body shimmering light. She turned corporeal long enough to slice off demon heads and disembowel anyone who got in her way.

They led the way, bowling through the demons and clearing the path. I caught sight of the Cats of Catastrophe rampaging through the demons. I hadn't realized they'd gotten outside the castle walls, but they clearly wanted to be in the middle of the fight.

"Get ready to clear out soon, cats!" I shouted.

Muffin meowed, indicating that he had heard me.

Next to me, Cass joined me in throwing fire at the demons. Her fireballs could take out six at a time.

Nix fired her bow and arrow faster than I had ever seen anyone use the weapon. Her aim was spectacular. Bree fought from the sky, sending lightning streaking down toward the demons. Thunder cracked in the air, a deafening soundtrack to the battle.

Once we reached the middle of the mass of demons, I dug into my pocket and pulled out Connor's bomb. "I'll hang off the back and lay it down." I looked at Cass. "Can you cover me with a massive fire wall so no demons can see me?"

She grinned. "On it."

"Be careful!" Rowan slowed the buggy as I climbed over the back seat.

Cass joined me on the back platform, raising her hands and creating a massive wall of fire at the back of the buggy. It gave me about ten feet of space to work in secret. I slipped over the railing and hung off, carefully putting the stone on the ground.

Cass's flame was hot and fierce, but it hid me from the eye of the demons. When the fire stopped, they probably wouldn't even notice the little rock on the ground.

I hauled myself back up onto the buggy, and Cass cut the flame.

"Go!" I shouted.

Rowan stepped on the gas, and the buggy surged forward. The demons closed in to fill the gap we'd left behind, but none of them seemed to notice the little rock on the ground. I prayed that none of them would kick it.

As we sped away from the bomb, Rowan veered the buggy left and right, picking up our friends, who still fought amongst the hordes.

I caught sight of Muffin, flying above the massive demons

and gouging out their eyes with his claws. "Muffin! Get out of here, and take the other cats. Now!"

He didn't need to be told twice. That cat knew when trouble was about to go down.

The cats raced off the battlefield, jumping from demon head to demon head like they were springboards, making record time.

I watched the horde of demons anxiously, waiting for the blast to go off.

When it came, it threw me backward on the platform. I slammed into the metal bars, and the buggy skidded to the side when Rowan lost control.

We slowed to a halt.

When I stood, the battlefield around us was chaos. Demon bodies were littered everywhere. A circle of demons remained around the perimeter, but they looked as disoriented as I felt. There were at least two hundred of them left, maybe three hundred. Toward the far side of the circle of demons, the Fates were rising to their feet. The blast had killed many of the demons around them, but they were too strong to be taken out by an explosion alone.

My friends leapt out of the buggy and charged the demons who stood in a massive circle. Protectorate members used ropes to rappel down the sides of the castle walls, then they streamed toward the demons. Connor must have told them my plan to destroy the Fates, and they were distracting the demons.

The battle erupted, my friends holding off the demons and giving me a chance to confront the Fates. The battle formed an arena of death, and I would be the main show.

I couldn't waste a single moment.

They just needed to keep the demons away long enough for me to attack the Fates. I looked up at the sky, imagining myself turning into the Battle Crow.

The transformation was instantaneous. One moment I was

standing, and the next I was in the air. I flew toward the sky as my friends' exclamations of shock echoed in my ears.

I flew straight for the Fates, determined to end this once and for all. I just needed to get in position, close enough to use my light power against them. It had killed the other Fate, and it would work against these two.

They saw me coming, and rage twisted their faces. Their armor gleamed in the light. Together, they hurled their sonic booms at me. I dived right, avoiding the masses of magic that would have thrown me out of the sky.

I swept down to attack, but they threw their sonic booms again. This time I wasn't so lucky. The edge of one of the booms hit me in the wing, and I tumbled in the sky, barely righting myself before plowing into the ground.

I flew upward, catching sight of Bree. She hovered in the sky, her silver wings glinting. "I'll take the one on the left and hold her off while you finish the other."

"Squawk!" Crap. I'd forgotten I couldn't talk in this form. But she seemed to get the message.

Bree's lightning struck toward the Fate on the left, and I flew toward the one on the right. All around, battle raged as my friends held off the demon attack, keeping them from throwing fire and magic to take me out of the sky.

As I approached, the Fate shouted curses at me, something ancient and foreign. But she wouldn't win this. I was the Morrigan, goddess of battle and fate. Or I had her powers, at least. I was on the side of right, and I would win.

I dodged her sonic booms, calling upon the magic within me. It blasted from me as a white light, fiercer than it had ever been. When I was in my Battle Crow form, my magic seemed stronger.

The light exploded in the air, hitting the Fate square in the chest. I poured it into her, forcing the goodness and light and hope toward evil. She shrieked in rage, then disappeared in a poof of dust.

I darted away, flying around the side in order to attack the last standing Fate. All around, the battle raged.

My friends kept the demons away from us, giving us time to fight. Bree sent lightning at the last Fate, all the while trying to dodge her sonic booms. I flew toward her, getting into position.

A fire ball slammed into my back from behind, pain igniting. One of the demons must've slipped through. I whirled on the air, and dived low, stabbing him through the eye with my beak.

Gross.

Instinct had driven me in my Battle Crow form, but human-me did not like the taste of eyeballs and brains. I tried to spit, vowing never to do that again, and flew high into the air, heading toward Bree.

The Fate turned her attention away from Bree and faced me, throwing her sonic boom. I dodged left, then right. But the third sonic boom hit me in in the leg, upsetting my balance on the air.

Pain flared as I tumbled through the air, heading toward the ground. I slammed into it, agony streaking through me.

Through bleary vision, I caught sight of the Fate racing toward me, her hands raised and rage on her face. I struggled to rise, to get back into the air, but she was so fast. If she hit me dead-on with another sonic boom, I could be dead.

"Hey!" Rowan's shriek came from behind the Fate. My gaze went toward her just in time to see her fire an arrow at the Fate.

The Fate turned, distracted from delivering a killing blow in my direction. The arrow slammed into her arm, and she howled.

I used the time to push off into the sky, flying high.

"Up here!" Bree shouted, distracting the Fate from Rowan.

She turned to look at Bree, so fast she was hard to see. She had to be the strongest one, and rage was fueling her movements. If someone had killed my sisters, I'd stop at nothing to get them in return.

Bree sent a crack of lightning directly toward the Fate. This time, the bolt shot straight into her. She shook and fell backward.

She was up seconds later, but Bree's lightning had given me just enough time to call upon my magic. I reached deep inside myself and let the light fill me, then pushed it outward toward the Fate.

More and more, I gave her everything I had. Hope and goodness and joy and life. Everything that she wasn't.

But I was running low. Even though I was stronger in this form, I'd used so much already.

I gasped, weakness invading my muscles, but kept pouring more magic toward the Fate.

I'd have to give her everything I had.

So I did.

I knew instinctively that it could kill me, but I did it.

I forced more magic into her, wringing it out of my very soul.

I envisioned *why* I was fighting. The faces of my friends, sisters, Lachlan. I couldn't let her win.

Finally, she shrieked and disappeared in a poof of dust. It was the last thing I heard before I fell from the sky.

16

"A na! Ana, wake up!" Strong hands shook my shoulders, and my eyes fluttered open.

The sounds of the battle had died down, so it took me a moment to realize why I was outside. Then it hit me. I looked down at my hand.

The tattoo was gone.

I looked up at Lachlan. "So we won?"

He pulled me close and pressed a quick kiss to my lips. "We won."

"Heck yeah." The last thing I remembered was falling out of the sky after killing the last Fate, but I didn't have any broken bones that I could feel. Just some aches from the sonic booms. "Did you catch me?"

"Barely." He grinned, then helped me stand.

All around, the bodies of the demons were disappearing. My sisters limped over, looking bruised and bloodied.

"So, you're a bird now," Bree said.

"Yep. Do you not remember me turning back time as the Battle Crow?"

She rubbed her head. "Maybe? It feels like a dream though. I can't be sure if it's right."

"Same." Rowan's brow furrowed, as if she were trying to remember.

That made sense. When I'd turned back time, I'd made it so that they'd never lived the moment when they'd seen me turn. But maybe some of their subconscious remembered. Somehow.

I turned my gaze toward the battlefield, looking for the rest of my friends. Everyone on the walls was cheering, thank fates, which I took to mean that there were no deaths back there. The demons had never breached the walls, apparently.

Though there were injuries on the battlefield, everyone was upright, staggering around and searching the demon bodies for valuables like transport charms.

Muffin fluttered over to me. *We did it!*

Princess Snowflake III and Bojangles followed, delight sparkling in their eyes. They loved a good battle.

"I think we did." I still couldn't believe it was over.

"I bet this means you'll graduate from the Academy." Bree grinned wide. "Saving the day tends to do that."

I smiled. That would be pretty good, actually. I had come into my power, after all. Hopefully Jude agreed that I'd earned it. Speaking of earned it. We needed a party.

I looked at my sisters and Lachlan. "I think we need to celebrate."

THE PARTY WENT down at the Whisky and Warlock pub later that night. Everyone's injuries were tended to and the defenses around the wall shored up.

By night time, we were all partying in the crowded little pub in the Grassmarket. Edinburgh was lit up at night, the lights twinkling outside of the windows.

Inside, the fire burned merrily, and most of the Protectorate members crowded around the little tables and chairs. All of the cursed tattoos were gone, and everyone was here. The Cats of Catastrophe had called a truce with the Pugs of Destruction for the evening, and they all sat in front of the warm fire. Muffin was making eyes at Kitty, the black cat who lived in the pub, and I wished him the best of luck. Even the FireSouls and their men had stayed, raising a glass to our victory against the Fates.

Sophie had given me a glass of bubbly pink champagne, while Bree drank her frothy pink cocktail called Witch's Rebellion. Rowan leaned into me and stole a sip of my drink.

"Hey, where's yours?"

She grinned. "Need a refill." She hugged me. "You did good, sis."

"Not bad, huh?" I was pretty pleased with how it had all turned out. No deaths made it a major victory. I turned to look at Lachlan. He sat next to me on the bench against the wall. "How are you doing?"

He wrapped an arm around me and tugged me closer to his side. "Perfect, now that I'm with you."

I snuggled closer to him. We hadn't had *The Talk* about where this was going, but it was clear it was about to get more serious. You didn't survive what we had, plus confess love, and not get more serious.

On the far side of the room, Lavender met my eyes and raised her glass. We might never be friends, but we were definitely more cordial now.

"Excuse me, everyone!" Jude's voice rose over the noise of partying Protectorate members. Her blue eyes sparkled and her dark skin glowed in the light of the fire. "I have an announcement to make."

The room quieted down, and everyone shifted forward, eager to hear what Jude had to say.

"We had a great victory today, thanks in no small part to one of our newest recruits, Ana Blackwood." She raised her glass to me. "Thank you, Ana. Quite simply, you saved the day."

Everyone cheered, glasses raised.

My heart warmed.

"You've come into your magic," Jude continued. "And accomplished something that few of our number ever have. As such, I'd like to announce that you have finished your time at the Academy and will be added to my unit, the Paranormal Investigative Team."

I grinned and looked at Bree. I'd be joining her team.

The crowd cheered as Jude finished her toast, but I didn't hear much more than that. I leaned closer to Lachlan and looked around the room, taking in the sight of my friends and allies.

I couldn't believe how far I'd come since my time in Death Valley, when my sisters and I had been scrabbling for a living. We'd found a real home here, and a family.

I reached for Bree and Rowan's hands and squeezed. I was the luckiest girl in the world.

THANK YOU FOR READING!

I hope you enjoyed this book as much as I enjoyed writing it. Reviews are *so* helpful to authors. If you want to leave one, you can do so on Amazon or GoodReads.

Want to know how Bree & company got started driving across Death Valley? Join my mailing list at www.linseyhall.com/subscribe to get a free copy of *Death Valley Magic*, the story of the Dragon Gods' early adventures. It is available only to newsletter subscribers. Turn the page for an excerpt.

EXCERPT OF DEATH VALLEY MAGIC

Death Valley Junction
  Eight years before the events in Undercover Magic

Getting fired sucked. Especially when it was from a place as crappy as the Death's Door Saloon.

"Don't let the door hit you on the way out," my ex-boss said.

"Screw you, Don." I flipped him the bird and strode out into the sunlight that never gave Death Valley a break.

The door slammed behind me as I shoved on my sunglasses and stomped down the boardwalk with my hands stuffed in my pockets.

What was I going to tell my sisters? We *needed* this job.

There were roughly zero freaking jobs available in this postage stamp town, and I'd just given one up because I wouldn't let the old timers pinch me on the butt when I brought them their beer.

Good going, Ana.

I kicked the dust on the ground and quickened my pace toward home, wondering if Bree and Rowan had heard from Uncle Joe yet. He wasn't blood family—we had none of that left besides each other—but he was the closest thing to it and he'd been missing for three days.

Three days was a lifetime when you were crossing Death Valley. Uncle Joe made the perilous trip about once a month, delivering outlaws to Hider's Haven. It was a dangerous trip on the best of days. But he should have been back by now.

Worry tugged at me as I made the short walk home. Death Valley Junction was a nothing town in the middle of Death Valley, the only all-supernatural city for hundreds of miles. It looked like it was right out of the old west, with low-slung wooden buildings, swinging saloon doors, and boardwalks stretching along the dirt roads.

Our house was at the end of town, a ramshackle thing that had last been repaired in the 1950s. As usual, Bree and Rowan were outside, working on the buggy. The buggy was a monster truck, the type of vehicle used to cross the valley, and it was our pride and joy.

Bree's sturdy boots stuck out from underneath the front of the truck, and Rowan was at the side, painting Ravener poison onto the spikes that protruded from the doors.

"Hey, guys."

Rowan turned. Confusion flashed in her green eyes, and she shoved her black hair back from her cheek. "Oh hell. What happened?"

"Fired." I looked down. "Sorry."

Bree rolled out from under the car. Her dark hair glinted in the sun as she stood, and grease dotted her skin where it was revealed by the strappy brown leather top she wore. We all wore the same style, since it was suited to the climate.

She squinted up at me. "I told you that you should have left that job a long time ago."

"I know. But we needed the money to get the buggy up and running."

She shook her head. "Always the practical one."

"I'll take that as a compliment. Any word from Uncle Joe?"

"Nope." Bree flicked the little crystal she wore around her neck. "He still hasn't activated his panic charm, but he should have been home days ago."

Worry clutched in my stomach. "What if he's wounded and can't activate the charm?"

Months ago, we'd forced him to start wearing the charm. He'd refused initially, saying it didn't matter if we knew he was in trouble. It was too dangerous for us to cross the valley to get him.

But that meant just leaving him. And that was crap, obviously.

We might be young, but we were tough. And we had the buggy. True, we'd never made a trip across, and the truck was only now in working order. But we were gearing up for it. We wanted to join Uncle Joe in the business of transporting outlaws across the valley to Hider's Haven.

He was the only one in the whole town brave enough to make the trip, but he was getting old and we wanted to take over for him. The pay was good. Even better, I wouldn't have to let anyone pinch me on the butt.

There weren't a lot of jobs for girls on the run. We could only be paid under the table, which made it hard.

"Even if he was wounded, Uncle Joe would find a way to activate the charm," Bree said.

As if he'd heard her, the charm around Bree's neck lit up, golden and bright.

She looked down, eyes widening. "Holy fates."

Panic sliced through me. My gaze met hers, then darted to Rowan's. Worry glinted in both their eyes.

"We have to go," Rowan said.

I nodded, my mind racing. This was *real*. We'd only ever

talked about crossing the valley. Planned and planned and planned.

But this was *go time*.

"Is the buggy ready?" I asked.

"As ready as it'll ever be," Rowan said.

My gaze traced over it. The truck was a hulking beast, with huge, sturdy tires and platforms built over the front hood and the back. We'd only ever heard stories of the monsters out in Death Valley, but we needed a place from which to fight them and the platforms should do the job. The huge spikes on the sides would help, but we'd be responsible for fending off most of the monsters.

All of the cars in Death Valley Junction looked like something out of *Mad Max*, but ours was one of the few that had been built to cross the valley.

At least, we hoped it could cross.

We had some magic to help us out, at least. I could create shields, Bree could shoot sonic booms, and Rowan could move things with her mind.

Rowan's gaze drifted to the sun that was high in the sky. "Not the best time to go, but I don't see how we have a choice."

I nodded. No one wanted to cross the valley in the day. According to Uncle Joe, it was the most dangerous of all. But things must be really bad if he'd pressed the button now.

He was probably hoping we were smart enough to wait to cross.

We weren't.

"Let's get dressed and go." I hurried up the creaky front steps and into the ramshackle house.

It didn't take long to dig through my meager possessions and find the leather pants and strappy top that would be my fight wear for out in the valley. It was too hot for anything more, though night would bring the cold.

Daggers were my preferred weapon—mostly since they were cheaper than swords and I had good aim with anything small and pointy. I shoved as many as I could into the little pockets built into the outside of my boots and pants. A small duffel full of daggers completed my arsenal.

I grabbed a leather jacket and the sand goggles that I'd gotten second hand, then ran out of the room. I nearly collided with Bree, whose blue eyes were bright with worry.

"We can do this," I said.

She nodded. "You're right. It's been our plan all along."

I swallowed hard, mind racing with all the things that could go wrong. The valley was full of monsters and dangerous challenges—and according to Uncle Joe, they changed every day. We had no idea what would be coming at us, but we couldn't turn back.

Not with Uncle Joe on the other side.

We swung by the kitchen to grab jugs of water and some food, then hurried out of the house. Rowan was already in the driver's seat, ready to go. Her sand goggles were pushed up on her head, and her leather top looked like armor.

"Get a move on!" she shouted.

I raced to the truck and scrambled up onto the back platform. Though I could open the side door, I was still wary of the Ravener poison Rowan had painted onto the spikes. It would paralyze me for twenty-four hours, and that was the last thing we needed.

Bree scrambled up to join me, and we tossed the supplies onto the floorboard of the back seat, then joined Rowan in the front, sitting on the long bench.

She cranked the engine, which grumbled and roared, then pulled away from the house.

"Holy crap, it's happening." Excitement and fear shivered across my skin.

Worry was a familiar foe. I'd been worried my whole life. Worried about hiding from the unknown people who hunted us. Worried about paying the bills. Worried about my sisters. But it'd never done me any good. So I shoved aside my fear for Uncle Joe and focused on what was ahead.

The wind tore through my hair as Rowan drove away from Death Valley Junction, cutting across the desert floor as the sun blazed down. I shielded my eyes, scouting the mountains ahead. The range rose tall, cast in shadows of gray and beige.

Bree pointed to a path that had been worn through the scrubby ground. "Try here!"

Rowan turned right, and the buggy cut toward the mountains. There was a parallel valley—the *real* Death Valley— that only supernaturals could access. That was what we had to cross.

Rowan drove straight for one of the shallower inclines, slowing the buggy as it climbed up the mountain. The big tires dug into the ground, and I prayed they'd hold up. We'd built most of the buggy from secondhand stuff, and there was no telling what was going to give out first.

The three of us leaned forward as we neared the top, and I swore I could hear our heartbeats pounding in unison. When we crested the ridge and spotted the valley spread out below us, my breath caught.

It was beautiful. And terrifying. The long valley had to be at least a hundred miles long and several miles wide. Different colors swirled across the ground, looking like they simmered with heat.

Danger cloaked the place, dark magic that made my skin crawl.

"Welcome to hell," Bree muttered.

"I kinda like it," I said. "It's terrifying but..."

"Awesome," Rowan said.

"You are both nuts," Bree said. "Now drive us down there. I'm ready to fight some monsters."

Rowan saluted and pulled the buggy over the mountain ridge, then navigated her way down the mountainside.

"I wonder what will hit us first?" My heart raced at the thought.

"Could be anything," Bree said. "Bad Water has monsters, kaleidoscope dunes has all kinds of crazy shit, and the arches could be trouble."

We were at least a hundred miles from Hider's Haven, though Uncle Joe said the distances could change sometimes. Anything could come at us in that amount of time.

Rowan pulled the buggy onto the flat ground.

"I'll take the back." I undid my seatbelt and scrambled up onto the back platform.

Bree climbed onto the front platform, carrying her sword.

"Hang on tight!" Rowan cried.

I gripped the safety railing that we'd installed on the back platform and crouched to keep my balance. She hit the gas, and the buggy jumped forward.

Rowan laughed like a loon and drove us straight into hell.

Up ahead, the ground shimmered in the sun, glowing silver.

"What do you think that is?" Rowan called.

"I don't know," I shouted. "Go around!"

She turned left, trying to cut around the reflective ground, but the silver just extended into our path, growing wider and wider. Death Valley moving to accommodate us.

Moving to trap us.

Then the silver raced toward us, stretching across the ground.

There was no way around.

"You're going to have to drive over it!" I shouted.

She hit the gas harder, and the buggy sped up. The reflective surface glinted in the sun, and as the tires passed over it, water kicked up from the wheels.

"It's the Bad Water!" I cried.

The old salt lake was sometimes dried up, sometimes not. But it wasn't supposed to be deep. Six inches, max. Right?

Please be right, Uncle Joe.

Rowan sped over the water, the buggy's tires sending up silver spray that sparkled in the sunlight. It smelled like rotten eggs, and I gagged, then breathed shallowly through my mouth.

Magic always had a signature—taste, smell, sound. Something that lit up one of the five senses. Maybe more.

And a rotten egg stink was bad news. That meant dark magic.

Tension fizzed across my skin as we drove through the Bad Water. On either side of the car, water sprayed up from the wheels in a dazzling display that belied the danger of the situation. By the time the explosion came, I was strung so tight that I almost leapt off the platform.

The monster was as wide as the buggy, but so long that I couldn't see where it began or ended. It was a massive sea creature with fangs as long as my arm and brilliant blue eyes. Silver scales were the same color as the water, which was still only six inches deep, thank fates.

Magic propelled the monster, who circled our vehicle, his body glinting in the sun. He had to be a hundred feet long, with black wings and claws. He climbed on the ground and leapt into the air, slithering around as he examined us.

"It's the Unhcegila!" Bree cried from the front.

Shit.

Uncle Joe had told us about the Unhcegila—a terrifying water monster from Dakota and Lakota Sioux legends.

Except it was real, as all good legends were. And it occasionally appeared when the Bad Water wasn't dried up. It only needed a few inches to appear.

Looked like it was our lucky day.

~~~

Join my mailing list at www.linseyhall.com/subscribe to continue the adventure and get a free ebook copy of *Death Valley Magic*. No spam and you can leave anytime!

AUTHOR'S NOTE

Thanks for reading *Doomsday Magic*! If you've read any of my previous books, you may have noticed that I have a fondness for including historical places and mythological elements. I did the same with *Doomsday Magic*. Sometimes the history of these things is so interesting that I want to share more, so I like to do it in the Author's Note instead of the story itself.

The story of the seal woman is one of my favorite parts of the book. It is based upon a folktale called the Legend of Kópakonan from the Faroe Islands, which are located far north of Scotland.

The Corryvreckan whirlpool is one of the largest natural whirlpools in the world. In real life, it's located off the west coast of Scotland. For the purposes of the story, I moved it to the north. The whirlpool is formed when the strong current that passes between the islands of Jura and Scarba meets the underwater topography of that area. A deep hole and a rising pinnacle create enough obstruction under the water that the whirlpool is formed.

The faces that Ana sees on the boats at the Demonville harbor are based on the eyes that can be found on the bows of ancient Greek ships. Many of the ships featured eyes, and they could be represented by paint or stone. One of the most famous shipwrecks, the Tektaş Burnu shipwreck from around 430 BCE, features stone eyes that were found at the shipwreck site. No one knows for sure what the eyes were for, though some scholars theorize they were the eyes of gods and meant to protect the ship.

You probably guessed that I used Dante's Inferno for inspiration in the hell scene. I tried to represent the levels of his hell accurately, but I did take some liberties. The caravan that crosses the sandstorm in level two is an example, as was the nice cave where they spent the night. And while I wrote Dante to be a crazy guy who sides with evil, I doubt that he actually was.

In part of the book, the words *terrible* and *great* resonate with Ana. I don't address it directly in the text, but the Morrigan's name can mean either of those things. The greatness part is obvious—she's a goddess, after all. But she could also preside over victories in battle. If she chose the side opposite yours, she was most definitely considered terrible.

I think that's it for the history and mythology in *Doomsday Magic*—at least the big things. I hope you enjoyed the book and will come back for Rowan's story!

ACKNOWLEDGMENTS

Thank you, Ben, for everything. There would be no books without you.

Thank you to Jena O'Connor and Lindsey Loucks for your excellent editing. Thank you to Eleonora, Ash P Reads, and Richard for your eagle eyes on errors. The book is immensely better because of you! Thank you to Jon McGough for recommending the Corryvreckan whirlpool as a cool element for a book.

Thank you to Orina Kafe for the beautiful cover art. Thank you to Collette Markwardt for allowing me to borrow the Pugs of Destruction, who are real dogs named Chaos, Havoc, and Ruckus. They were all adopted from rescue agencies.

GLOSSARY

Alpha Council - There are two governments that enforce law for supernaturals—the Alpha Council and the Order of the Magica. The Alpha Council governs all shifters. They work cooperatively with the Alpha Council when necessary—for example, when capturing FireSouls.

Blood Sorcerer - A type of Magica who can create magic using blood.

Dark Magic - The kind that is meant to harm. It's not necessarily bad, but it often is.

Demons - Often employed to do evil. They live in various hells but can be released upon the earth if you know how to get to them and then get them out. If they are killed on Earth, they are sent back to their hell.

Dragon God - A rare Magica who was created by gods and dragons. They each represent a mythical pantheon.

Djinn - Possesses invisibility and the ability to possess others for brief periods of time.

Earthwalking Gods - Reincarnates of the ancient gods who can walk upon the earth. They are mortal but with all the power of that god.

Elders of the Indomidae - An ancient magical sect that lives in the far North Sea.

Enchanted Artifacts – Artifacts can be imbued with magic that lasts after the death of the person who put the magic into the artifact (unlike a spell that has not been put into an artifact—these spells disappear after the Magica's death). But magic is not stable. After a period of time—hundreds or thousands of years depending on the circumstance—the magic will degrade. Eventually, it can go bad and cause many problems.

Fire Mage – A mage who can control fire.

FireSoul - A very rare type of Magica who shares a piece of the dragon's soul. They can locate treasure and steal the gifts (powers) of other supernaturals. With practice, they can manipulate the gifts they steal, becoming the strongest of that gift. They are despised and feared. If they are caught, they are thrown in the Prison of Magical Deviants.

The Great Peace - The most powerful piece of magic ever created. It hides magic from the eyes of humans.

Magica - Any supernatural who has the power to create magic—witches, sorcerers, mages. All are governed by the Order of the Magica.

Order of the Magica - There are two governments that enforce law for supernaturals—the Alpha Council and the Order of the Magica. The Order of the Magica govern all Magica. They work cooperatively with the Alpha Council when necessary—for example, when capturing FireSouls.

Seeker - A type of supernatural who can find things. Fire-Souls often pass off their dragon sense as Seeker power.

Shifter - A supernatural who can turn into an animal. All are governed by the Alpha Council.

Transporter - A type of supernatural who can travel anywhere. Their power is limited and must regenerate after each use.

Undercover Protectorate - A secret organization dedicated to protecting supernaturals and solving the crimes that no one else will.

Vampire - Blood drinking supernaturals with great strength and speed who live in a separate realm.

ABOUT LINSEY

Before becoming a writer, Linsey Hall was a nautical archaeologist who studied shipwrecks from Hawaii and the Yukon to the UK and the Mediterranean. She credits fantasy and historical romances with her love of history and her career as an archaeologist. After a decade of tromping around the globe in search of old bits of stuff that people left lying about, she settled down and started penning her own romance novels. Her Dragon's Gift series draws upon her love of history and the paranormal elements that she can't help but include.

COPYRIGHT

Copyright 2018 by Linsey Hall
Published by Bonnie Doon Press LLC

Linsey@LinseyHall.com
www.LinseyHall.com
https://www.facebook.com/LinseyHallAuthor
ISBN 978-1-942085-59-1